ANGEL KILLS

Remi DeWitt

UK Book Publishing.com

Design, typesetting and publishing by UK Book Publishing

www.ukbookpublishing.com

ISBN: 978-1-916572-01-0

Cover photo by *Andrey Zvyagintsev* on *Unsplash*

ANGEL
KILLS

CHAPTER ONE

M en are simple creatures. Easy to manipulate, except when they're ignoring you. This one is ignoring me now. He's craggy, graying at the edges, and wearing a very expensive suit. Lean and commanding, he expects to be obeyed, and he is. Sitting on either side of him in that booth are two of his brigadiers. They're probably in their thirties, also expensively suited, and hanging on his every word. Someone who didn't know better might think they'd come straight from Wall Street. There's nothing like some top-shelf booze in an exclusive club when you're talking about whose savings you've just wiped out. These guys are in the business of wiping out other things, like teeth. Give them each a uniform and a hammer and they would've fit right in at the Lubyanka.

This isn't the Lubyanka. This is a nightclub. The dance floor is wide, with booths all around except for the long bar to my right. A guy sits behind it with a smoke in one hand and a thick, thick novel in the other, probably one of those interminable Russian masterpieces. Above is a balcony.

Later on, from somewhere up there, the DJ will rock the joint. For now, it's shrouded in darkness.

This is one of the reasons why clubs are not my favorite places: too many shadowy corners where anything could be happening. There's also the noise and the crowd. These things matter. In my business, a botched quick exit is always just one wrong step away. At least this early in the evening the place is all but empty, hollow, and dead, like some gutted corpse. If it had a smell it would reek of cynicism, exploitation, and take as much as you can get. Deplorable, despicable, detestable . . . or maybe that's just the way it is. Business is business, after all, and a girl's gotta make a buck the same as any *boyevik*.

Several of them are hanging around waiting to be told what to do. They sit in booths in twos and threes. Their low conversation broke off as they watched me clack across the dance floor. Now they're back to talking with occasional bursts of laughter, although some of them are still sneaking a peek. That's okay. You drink it in, guys. You all know that's as close as you're ever going to get.

At last, the conversation ends. The two brigadiers get up and leave and their *pakhan* finally decides to notice. After looking me over for a moment, he smiles and says in English so good you can hardly hear his Russian accent, "This is good. I like this dress. I think it suits you very well."

So you should. The blonde wig, the sparkly, red dress, the chunky jewelry: none of them are my idea of chic. It's all for you, sweetness. So enjoy.

"Please. Sit."

I squeeze into the booth beside him, placing my purse between us on the bench. It's dark-red leather, all buttoned up and very plush. The table we're at is knee-level frosted glass. It's lit from underneath, like everything else in here. Someone somewhere must have thought making your patrons look ghoulish was some kind of cool. A real goth would probably look at it and curl a long-suffering lip.

A wave of his hand brings two shot glasses and a bottle of vodka: the genuine article, straight from Mother Russia, with a label printed in Cyrillic and everything. All that's missing are some salty snacks. He's probably thinking we'll be getting to that later.

"You like vodka?" He's not expecting an answer. "So we drink. Then we go somewhere a little more private." After we've savored the smoothness of the burn, he adds, "I am Grigori, but she told you that, yes?"

His gaze is intense, intended to unsettle, but then so is mine. There's no room for flinching here, as our mutual acquaintance discovered when she tried to deny me. She's a sweet lady who lives on the other side of town. Her neighbors don't know it, but she runs a string of girls on the internet. Grigori is one of her best customers, and she didn't want to give him to me. The stare soon changed her mind; that, and being asked if the cops knew about her little enterprise. Sometimes a dime can be as persuasive as a bullet.

"Good. She never disappoints. I like working with people who don't disappoint."

It certainly beats being left in the lurch. My own Mr. Reliable is waiting outside. The goons on the door wouldn't let him in. It doesn't matter. Grigori isn't going to be a problem.

"You do not speak? At least tell me what I should call you."

"Yekaterina. I am Yekaterina."

Hearing my own faint Russian accent, he thinks he knows me. *"Russkaya. Zdravstvuyte, devushka.* So you came to this country because they promised you a better life, yes? Perhaps you should tell me their names. If you please me, maybe I will have them killed for you." He smiles mirthlessly. "Unless they work for me, of course."

"Because you are Volkov, the wolf, and wolves never kill their own."

"I am Volkov. But you are wrong. Wolves do sometimes kill their own, or cast them out. *Nye bespokoysya.* Do not worry. Tonight, the wolves are resting."

Or not. One of his brigadiers returns. He leans down to whisper into Grigori's ear. Grigori listens, his expression hardening with every word. He replies with a wagging finger and a final chop of the hand. The brigadier straightens, nods, and marches away. Looks like there's a wolf out there who's about to be cast out—if he's lucky.

It's no business of mine, but it is time to move my own business along. In my purse is a little silver pillbox, embossed with pretty flowers and such. The goon who searched me on the way in tried to open it. He couldn't. That's my little secret.

"*Ladna.*" Grigori is all smiles again. "So, what were we talking about?"

A thin layer of felt covers the base of the pillbox. Beneath it is a film of stickiness. "Tonight the wolves are resting, but still the shepherd watches, I think."

"Of course. It is a foolish shepherd who sleeps when there are more than wolves out there. Now smile for me, Katya. You are too beautiful to always be so serious."

What he wants, he gets. Besides, a pretty smile is as good as tears for putting them off their guard. "I am sorry, but now you will excuse me, yes? I need to go fix my makeup. I will only be a moment, I promise."

So is a kiss, just a quick peck on the cheek that buys his patience. At the same time, the pillbox sticks nicely to the back of his jacket, just above his shoulder blades. So long as he doesn't stand up, no one will notice. The clattering of my heels across the dance floor has all those greedy eyes watching again. They're too busy drinking in my booty to notice the burner phone. Just a few more steps to safety and speed dial detonates an ounce or so of the biggest bang a buck can buy. Poor Grigori. He was a foolish shepherd after all.

Dead silence follows, without even the sound of my heels breaking it on the carpeting of the stairs. There's no need to hurry. They haven't even begun to figure out what the hell just happened.

Out in the chilly night air, the two goons are still standing there with their hands clasped in front of them. They don't appear to have noticed the small bomb that just went off inside. Well, this is a club. Maybe it's soundproofed. They'll hear about it soon enough, but by then, the deadliest bang in town will have disappeared into the night.

My minder is waiting for me on the sidewalk. With the door to my ride open and my coat held out, ready for me to slip into it, he greets me with a nod. "We good?"

"We're good." He doesn't know what just went down either. It's not his business to know. So maybe it's my sudden return that's got him asking. "Some guys just can't contain themselves, y'know? One kiss and they're all over the place."

"Yeah, I got a brother like that. His head just turns to mush at the sight of a pretty face. So, where to now?"

"Grand Central. We have some time to kill, so take the scenic route."

It's doubtful anyone in that club will think to follow us, but there's no such thing as being too careful.

One mini-tour of Manhattan later, through all the bright lights and busy streets where no one knows my name, and my guy is paid off handsomely. He's such a cutie and so very, very good, he deserves a little extra. With our business done, he disappears into the evening traffic and a cab takes me home. Something less gaudy is waiting, already laid out on the bed, because that dinner reservation is in fifteen minutes. It's my little way of rewarding myself for a job well done.

CHAPTER ONE

***

"Hey." He sits down opposite me like he's been invited. It's lunchtime, and a quick glance around the coffee shop shows me it's quite busy, but even so.

He smiles—a big, fat, I'm-the-guy-you've-been-waiting-for kinda smile. Sorry, pal. With that slick New York grooming and all, you might think you're irresistible, but you look like just another wiseass on the make to me.

"So." Oozing confidence like honey from a comb, he doesn't even notice me not being swept off my feet. "You always wear your hair that short or are you one of those I-don't-need-a-man types?"

My own lunch is almost over. Leaving him cold is an option. He does have nice eyes though, smiling eyes, the kind of eyes that might surprise me with tickets to a show or a weekend in a high-end spa. He can have a few minutes of my time, just to show me what he's got. "Why? You looking for something to grab a hold of after you've clubbed me over the head?"

"No. I think it suits you, the way you got that whole boyish look going on. Short hair, no makeup, hazel eyes; man, I'm just melting like ice cream on a sidewalk. I'm Joey, by the way."

He holds out a hand. It's as perfectly manicured as the rest of him; with a good, firm grip. No matter how tightly he holds mine though, he's not getting my real name out of me. "Ellie. Thanks for the company, but I gotta go. Some of us have work to get back to, y'know."

"Hey, I hear you." He rises with me, which is sort of annoying. "I got places to be too. So how about you let me walk you?"

"Thanks, but you don't even know where I work."

Right now he's not the only one, but it seems nothing is going to deter him. "What's the world coming to if a gentleman can't find a few minutes out of his day to escort a lady safely to wherever she wants to go? Come on. I'm one of the good guys. Can't you see how my mom raised me right?"

"Yeah, I can see that." Except for the not taking no for an answer bit. "Well, it's a free country. You can walk wherever you want."

Out on the sidewalk we stroll through the crowd, passing by stores and cafes. None of them fills the bill, giving him more time to work his charms on me. "That's a nice little place. You go there every day?"

"No. I like to try different places." And that place certainly won't be seeing me again. "Y'know, mix it up a bit. Variety is the spice of life and all that."

"But you work around here, right?"

"Why? Did my few minutes suddenly run out or something?"

His grin turns wry. "You're not gonna make this easy, are you? That's okay. I like complicated. Simple is just so meh, don't you think?"

"Oh, I do." My deep, meaningful stare only makes him laugh. "Yeah, you're complicated. So what does a complicated lady do when she's not working or eating lunch?"

"Same as everyone else, I guess. Read, stream, surf: especially the news. I like to keep up on current events." Especially after a hit. It's been more than a week since Grigori. He's gone missing. The authorities suspect foul play. I suspect that's all they'll ever know.

"Figures. I didn't peg you for a reality TV kinda gal."

We're still passing by stores and cafes. If something doesn't come along soon, Mr. Perception here is going to unravel way too much of my carefully constructed anonymity. "I'm guessing you're not the sporty type either. Too many novels no one else can understand just waiting to be read, right."

"I read a lot more than novels no one else can understand. Perhaps you ought to try it sometime. And I do an hour in the gym every morning, if that's what you mean by sporty. Girl's gotta keep those pounds off; otherwise, how'll she get to meet a guy like you?"

"Dunno. I guess you just get lucky."

We come to a gallery. It's the kind of place my afternoons are browsed away in anyway, along with stores, libraries, and museums. This one has just become my place of employment. "Well, thanks for the company. Maybe we'll bump into each other again sometime."

"You never know. I always kinda thought I should get interested in art, like what's the difference between a Manet and a Monet. An *a* and an *o*, right. Yes? No? Okay, not funny. Seriously though, maybe you could give me some pointers.

Y'know, what might be a good investment and what not; that sort of thing. I'm thinking some candlelight and wine, a nice, out-of-the-way restaurant, our own private booth—"

"Bye."

Before he can answer, the door is closing behind me and my coat is off, just to make it look convincing. He watches through the window, his poor little face all full of hurt like he just had his heart broken. Aww, poor thing. If he comes in and starts begging for my number, one will be made up, followed by a quick disappearance before he finds himself talking to a total stranger, and a New York one at that. More likely, he's thinking he'll come back tomorrow and pick up where he left off. It's a good call because now he flashes his super-white smile at me and walks away.

Okay, he's not a complete dork, but the complications don't even bear thinking about, like, "Hi, Mom. Hi, Dad. This is my fiancée. Yeah, she's a contract killer . . . at least until we have kids."

With Joey gone, my daily routine gets back on track. After a couple hours of browsing—a bookstore, a place selling scented candles, whatever takes my fancy—it's time to buy groceries. They're whole food, of course, fresh and free from, because eating right matters, and who knows what those big corporations put in their processed garbage. A place in Tribeca is today's choice. It's not too far from my apartment and an easy walk home until BANG, my groceries are all over the sidewalk. Disbelief hardly covers it. As if Joey wasn't bad enough, my routine, my entire day, has just been ruined. "What the hell? Are you blind or did I just suddenly become invisible?"

His answer is a silent gaze as if he thinks those big, gooey eyes are going to shame me. He's also filthy, from the top of his stained hoodie to the bottom of his fraying sneakers. Strands of greasy hair frame his thin face while his mouth is surrounded by the poor, pathetic wisps of something that's trying to be facial hair. The same height as me, he's barely more than a wisp himself; so slight the merest breeze might blow him away. It's all so perfectly helpless, like a little, lost puppy that just wants to be loved. Nice try, kid, but you're not getting off that easy.

"Well! Don't just stand there. Pick it all up!"

Still saying nothing, he does exactly as he's told, stuffing everything back into the now-broken bag and hugging it to his filthy chest. Ugh!

Suddenly, the very thought of cooking and eating what's inside is stomach-churning. My routine is already ruined, so maybe I'll bin the lot and eat out tonight. It all still needs to be carried home though, in that broken bag, and it's certainly not going to be me doing it. Not while he's standing there being so wonderfully helpful.

"So! Come on, then!"

With him following a few paces behind, my mood begins to change. There is something quite delicious about knowing there's a boy walking behind me who could probably be ordered to do almost anything and he'd likely do it. My steps are lighter, my grin smirkier—until my phone chirps. My very private phone.

It's a text. There's no need for me to look. My next contract is waiting. It also brings me to my senses because this thing that's happening right now is really, really stupid. There's a stray dog following me: mangy, ragged, likely riddled with fleas and possibly rabid, and very soon about to know where I live.

By the time we reach Canal, this temporary insanity has passed. He's come as close to my apartment as he's going to get.

"Give me the bag."

Again, wordlessly, he obeys, and those eyes assault me for the second time. Joey had smiling eyes, almost but not quite good enough to have me melting like ice cream on a sidewalk. This one has eyes filled with sorrow and hurt like he's lost something he can never get back. It really is all so puppyish and begging for love that he almost does have me melting because everyone loves puppies, right? Wrong. No one's taking in anyone's wretched refuse today. A couple of bucks should more than cover it.

"Here, take it. Now go on. Go!"

He slouches away with a hangdog look over his shoulder. Still, it tugs at me. In case it's tugging at him too, a brief detour around a couple of blocks with frequent glances over my shoulder is enough to make sure he's not following me. Lonely little puppies will do that, and I don't have time to waste on lost causes. There's a contract in need of planning.

CHAPTER TWO

D C just got itself another tourist. Tourist is good. Tourist is a baseball cap and a coat tied around my waist. Tourist is wandering around looking vaguely lost with no one asking questions. Tourist is photographing the shit out of government buildings like I've never seen one before, all the while waiting for the mark to appear.

There are special instructions for this one. Follow him to wherever he goes when he skips out for lunch. Kill him and whoever he meets up with. That sounds an awful lot like a jilted wife to me—a very rich jilted wife if she can afford my services.

Just before midday, and exactly to schedule, he appears. He's an early lunch kinda guy, and he's also in a hurry. A block away, he jumps in a cab and disappears into traffic. Well, great. The instructions never said anything about following him out into the suburbs. Never mind. DC just got itself another cyclist, while the tourist fills the rest of her day with a visit to the Smithsonian.

Day two and the bike is a hire. The shorts, shirt, and helmet are all bought. Midday arrives and he doesn't appear. The rest of the week it's the same. Looks like cab guy just doesn't eat lunch that often. On the upside, that leaves my afternoons free for working up a good sweat.

Day seven and at last cab guy hurries out. I follow at a safe distance, pumping my way through the traffic as I keep him just in sight. Eventually, we arrive in a nice, quiet suburb: trimmed and leafy, with immaculate lawns and lace-filled windows. He pays off the cab and bounds up to the front door of an ordinary-looking house. Someone immediately lets him in. Naughty boy. He has been playing away and now he's gonna pay for it.

The street both ways is empty. This is when it has to go down or it's another seven days of changing hotels. In my backpack is a .38 with a silencer attached. Supplied by a local contact, it's still in the box it was delivered in, all nicely printed up with the name of the company that delivered it. At a moment's notice, a courier will do as well as anything.

On the porch, my pretend knock goes unanswered. There's no one watching the door. Cab guy and whoever let him in are alone in there. The street is still empty, but it can't hurt to make it look like my time is being wasted. The door round the back is unlocked because who would burglarize this neighborhood in the middle of the day, right?

I step inside with the .38 leading the way. Beyond is the kitchen: all oak, chrome, and white tiles, and spotlessly clean. Nice. After that are the dining room, living room, and what looks like an office. Not too chintzy, not too cluttered. Clearly expensive. Someone with a bit of class decorated this place.

As I start up the stairs, the sound of a woman's voice begins to drift down to me. She's got a beef about something. Maybe he's been two-timing her as well. On the landing, the door is ajar. The .38 pushes it open, and then both me and my piece freeze. The walls are all mirrors. So is the ceiling. There are no windows. The only light is cast by a number of tall, black candles spaced around the edge of the floor. The woman is standing in the center of the room, almost facing me. She's wearing red: seriously heeled boots, stockings, a corset, and a high-collared cape. She's also wearing two chains around her neck: one with an upside-down cross, the other a set of keys. The keys must be for the chains and straps with which cab guy is bound before her. He's on his knees, his mouth filled with the supersized strap-on she's wearing, his head going back and forth like a pigeon on meth.

The woman sees me. "Who the hell—"

Two in the chest shuts her down. As she crumples in front of cab guy, he turns to look at me. Strangely, his eyes fill with a certain understanding. "No. Wait. I can—"

A little moral outrage seems appropriate right now.

"Really? You wanna suck the devil's cock in between criminalizing the rest of us? Well, frat boy, say hello to the angel of death."

I pump two into him, then one more in the head for each of them just to be sure, and the job is almost done. All that remains is to protect me. Some of these women like to video things by way of insurance, or as a future nest egg. Starring in a snuff movie isn't going to help my career one little bit so from top to bottom, the place gets trashed, with valuables taken along the way. If there is any recording equipment, it's too well hidden for me to find. A home invasion turned nasty is still good cover though.

Outside, the street is still empty. If someone is watching, a courier came and a courier went. There must be hundreds of them in DC. My exit is good.

***

The next morning in the departure lounge, the TVs say nothing about a double murder in the suburbs. There's just some corrupt politician claiming it was the other side who rigged a vote or molested an intern or some such. Perhaps they haven't discovered it yet. Cab guy was very careful to keep his satanic tryst a secret. Someone will notice soon enough. The woman must have had other clients, and government employees don't just disappear. Not that there's anything for me to worry about. Even if someone did see me, all the cops will have is some anonymous bike courier.

Back in New York, my routine embraces me like coming home to momma, except now momma has a ghost. He's a wisp of a boy in a dirty hoodie and frayed sneakers, and he haunts the sidewalk, his back seen in the middle of a crowd ahead of me or glimpsed turning a corner but never there by the time I've reached it. He is everywhere but nowhere, with eyes on the back of my neck but always imagined once I've turned.

This is ridiculous. This is obsessive. This is a cat lady looking for waifs and strays to fill a hole in her life. Why this should be is a mystery. He carried my groceries partway home and he was paid for it; that's all. There's nothing owed here. There's no room in my carefully constructed routine for such distractions.

But still, it's those eyes—deep wells of brown filled with that inconsolable sorrow. Goddammit, they're like heroin, always there at the back of my mind no matter how much I try to kick the habit.

A few days later, and cab guy is front-page news, but not a double murder in the suburbs. It seems he was some administration high-up who died unexpectedly of an embolism. Here are all his friends and coworkers saying what a wonderful guy he was and what a loss to the country he is. He might even have been president one day. Here's his family's lawyer, telling everyone that he leaves behind a wife and two children, a son and a daughter. They are deeply shocked at his sudden passing and ask that their privacy be respected. Yeah, she's as deeply shocked as me, and probably already eyeing up the pool guy. There's no mention of his devil-worshipping mistress. That's understandable. No Brahmin would want that plastered all over the media. All the same, it was a hit and they're covering it up. This one goes on the watch list, just in case.

***

Another day, another news item, but it's not cab guy. The story has been dropped. I wonder why. That lie about an embolism proves they know it was a hit. They're not going to just let that go. Who knows where it might end: anarchy, revolution, the loss of their status, power, and privilege. Someone somewhere is probably getting their ass kicked. Don't tell me no one saw anything. Turn stones over, kick doors in, arrest suspects. And if they won't talk, well, that's what we have black sites for, right? Good luck with that, guys. Nothing says job well done like all those government agencies lined up like ducks, all of them gliding serenely across the surface while their feet paddle furiously beneath.

After some more browsing, it's time to head out for lunch, and I'm feeling decidedly smirky. There might even be a treat involved.

It's a good afternoon, relaxed and carefree, with even those eyes forgotten—until there they are. He's standing in the middle of the sidewalk staring at me, almost as if he's been waiting for this. That ought to concern me, but one look into those eyes and everything is forgotten, like all those reasons for simply walking on by. My independence, my anonymity, everything that keeps me safe, they all become birds set free, their wings beating as they rise into the air. That sorrow, that loss, that puppy dog begging for love, and my inner cat lady becomes a Valkyrie, charging headlong into death or glory. There's nothing that's going to stop her from thrusting my groceries at him with a determined, "Take these!"

He does so wordlessly, once more following a few paces behind and kept that way with occasional words of encouragement, like, "Come on. Keep up—," and "Stay. Wait for the traffic. All right, come on."

Puppy learns fast and Valkyrie cat lady is tripping out on the wonderful thing she's doing until he's followed me all the way home, right up into my apartment.

"Over there!"

Pointed towards the open-plan kitchen, he obeys, placing the groceries on a worktop. Now that we're here, it's time to stand back and properly take in the state of him. That state has to be close to quite the most disgusting thing that's ever been scraped off a sidewalk. It's not just the dirt and the raggedness—or the smell that's snuck in with him. It's also the thought that he might have brought some uninvited guests with him, like lice. That's how stupid this is. If this had been work it, would have been thought through again and again until it was right. Instead, this is an impulse, a silly whim, and now those eyes are looking at me, and throwing him out just isn't an option.

Okay. The first thing to do is obvious. I pick up a trash bag along the way, because no way is any part of me touching those rags, and lead him to the nearest bathroom. "Take those filthy things off. Put them in this and take a shower."

He undresses. It's not a pretty sight. Besides, as I close the door on it, there's another problem to be solved. He's not putting those things on again because they're going straight down the chute, but he has to wear something. My apartment is minimalist, white-walled and uncluttered. The kitchen and living area are open-plan, with a balcony above stacked with books: my library. There are two bathrooms and four bedrooms. One of those bedrooms is my gym. Another two are used as closets. They are full of clothes, from designer to thrift store. This isn't compulsive buying. This is cover. A lawyer one day might be a bag lady the next, and whoever saw a bag lady wearing lawyer's shoes?

The search through them is quick enough; there are day dresses and suits with pants or skirts suitable for the office. There are ball gowns and party dresses, and naughty little dresses for playing the slut. There is everything that might be needed for whatever role has to be played. The one thing there isn't is any men's—

Suddenly, there's a devil sitting on my left shoulder and an angel sitting on my right, and the devil is saying, "You can," and the angel is saying, "You can't." And the devil is saying, "Oh, yes, you can," and the angel is saying, "No, no, no, you can't." And the third voice in my head, mine, is saying, "The hell with it. This is my apartment and I'll do what I want. If he's going to stay, he can damn well earn his keep, and he might as well be properly dressed for it too."

The little black maid's uniform comes off the rod, a naughty temptress that already has me feeling playful as it slips through the bathroom door. "Put this on when you're done."

Back in the kitchen, a very large glass of wine is poured. Never a big drinker, this is not my normal behavior. Ah, what the hell. The devil's already made a down payment on my soul.

A big, comfy leather chair in the living area is next. This is where one of those novels no one else can understand curls up with me for a quiet evening in. Thanks for putting that thought indelibly into my head, Joey. Today, it's that big glass of wine I'm curling up with. Also, a 9mm is resting on my thigh because cat lady has been put back in her box. Another Valkyrie is calling the shots now and there aren't going to be any discussions about it.

He's taking his time. Either it's a very long shower or he's summoning up the courage to appear in that uniform. My glass is refilled. It's almost empty again by the time he appears. When he does, there's just no helping it. He looks so utterly ridiculous that my snort of derision almost chokes me on the last of my wine.

The 9mm waves a little circle, ordering him to turn around. He obeys, and my playfulness begins to grow. What this needs are some falsies and stuff because my maid is going to fill out his uniform properly. In fact, we're doing it now.

While he refills my glass, my laptop fires up. A third glass of wine appears next to me. It begins to empty quickly, but this is way too much fun to be worrying about things like that. Very soon, we have what we need, even if he doesn't know it yet: silicone breast forms, mastectomy bras, and padded girdles. They'll be delivered tomorrow. He'll look supercute in them.

For now, he has returned to standing there, a boy in a dress. Most of the way through my third glass, my playfulness is turning into pure wickedness.

"Say something."

He doesn't.

"That's not very nice. Here I am bringing you home with me, cleaning you up, and dressing you all nice, and you won't even say thank you."

He stares at the floor. My grin must be pure evil by now.

"Oh my. I think there's a puppy who needs to be house-trained."

The 9mm waves about in my hand. My empty glass is thrust forward in the other.

"Fill this. Now."

He hurries to take it. While he's in the kitchen with his back to me, my wickedness is stripping me from the waist down. If he won't say how grateful he is, he can damn well show it another way. Sprawling in the chair with my legs half-open, the 9mm is hovering like the head of a cobra. When he returns, glass in hand, my legs begin to slowly widen. "Why, thank you, sweetie. But I still think you ought to show me some love. Come on now. Show me some big, sloppy love."

He doesn't even try to object.

CHAPTER THREE

I'm curled up in the middle of my bed, and the smell of coffee is slowly working its way between the sheets. He must be making breakfast. After what happened last night, that's weird. As to exactly what did happen, everything is crystal clear. He did not sleep in my bed. I did not have sex with that maid. Really. Even if he is now making breakfast like it's the morning after.

With that out of the way, the next question has to be dealt with. Drunk me did something really stupid. Sober me now has to clean up the mess. He knows my face. He knows my address. A lot of people who knew me on my way up ended up facedown in an alley simply for knowing things like that.

There are only two options. Either he stays, or he's taken down to the waterfront and gets a bullet through the head. No one's going to notice another dead street kid. Except, right now, this is way too hard to be thinking about. This needs a clear head, not one that's lying here wishing the sun wasn't streaming in through the window with a big rise-and-shine smile on its fat, round, and very smug face.

Crawling out of bed proves to be my next mistake. Oh . . . my . . . God! Forget clear head. That last glass of wine was way too many; so was the one before. Orange juice and coffee like a desert needs rain and make it quick, please.

A little silk robe lies nearby. It's red and green and white and something. Whatever. This is no time to be worrying about what to wear, especially when my feet are padding like elephants toward the living area. The buzzer for the apartment block door goes off. Damn! You're not waking the dead, y'know. Well, not yet anyway. It's a delivery. My head is way too muzzy to even begin to wonder what that might be.

The guy arrives at my front door with a box. Once it's been signed for, it goes into the kitchen where it's slit open with the first thing that comes to hand. Inside are breast forms, mastectomy bras, and padded girdles. The wall stares back at me. Someone ordered these when they were drunk. Someone did some other things too. Okay. Maybe my memory of last night isn't quite so crystal clear. No one slept in my bed but me though, and that's not up for discussion.

He's standing over there in a corner, hands folded in front of his little maid's apron as he waits to be told what to do. Now that he's all cleaned up, his beauty is starting to show. Forget cat lady; a cougar is stirring inside me. In the haze of that morning sunlight, he is almost pre-Raphaelite. All that's missing are the tumbling curls and the floaty gown. Well, maybe later. For now, all this drunken shopping stuff suddenly makes perfect sense. "Here! Go get dressed properly."

Watching him leave, it's not lost on me that he still hasn't said a word. Either he's refusing to or he's mute. Mute would certainly go a long way toward explaining why he's on the street. We'll deal with that later because right now breakfast is waiting, and it's perfectly laid out: orange juice, bran, French toast, and coffee. How he knows this is part of my routine, except for missing my morning workout, is a mystery. Maybe he just went with what was in the cupboards.

Breakfast has me just about ready to face the day, starting with my laptop. A trawl through the news and it's all just the usual believe what we tell you to believe. Shopping next: but this time not for bargains. Today's search is for a stylist/beautician: upmarket, will home visit, and, if offered enough, will fit me in this morning. I find one. Just a little over an hour later, she is standing next to me. We are both looking at Puppy, nicely plumped out in his new breasts and hips. She doesn't look at all happy; the expression on her face looking an awful lot like, "Really?"

She could be about to quit, as if she's not already being paid enough, but a little gentle shaming should take care of that. "What's the matter? You're not transphobic, are you? Because that would be just so deplorable. Imagine if that got out, and you with a business to run."

"Honey, I work all over this town. You wouldn't believe some of the things I've been asked to do. Boys wanna be girls, girls wanna be boys. I got no problem with any of that. I just hope you ain't expecting me to wax his balls, that's all. Because there are some things I ain't doing."

Well, there's no fault in saying it like it is. Until she brought it up, it hadn't even occurred to me. "You get asked to do that a lot?"

"All the time, and some of them are real pushy about it too. I tell ya, some people out there seem to think they got the right to demand whatever they want and I'm somehow supposed to just give it to 'em. Whatever happened to my right to refuse, huh? Or don't I got rights anymore?"

"Okay. So no ball waxing then, assuming you still want the job, of course?"

She does. We take him to the bathroom. There she sets about washing his hair, adding highlights, perming, and volumizing. The transformation has hardly even begun and yet it is wonderful, with the cougar inside me just wishing his hair was longer, like, halfway down his back.

To my bedroom next, where she waxes and threads him. As she begins to apply makeup, suddenly my desire for him darkens, clouding with a siren's call that's as dangerous as it is beguiling. She sings of things that were buried long ago, of betrayal, rage, and hate. They are the dead who must not rise; the underlying and never acknowledged reason for my self-control. They are the rock that must be avoided, even as the vision of purity he is becoming calls me toward it.

The kitchen becomes my refuge, with a glass of water in my hand that's hardly noticed. The dead are stirring, their ghosts trying to inhabit the blank wall in front of me. They want to ask me why. They want to tell me they did the best they could. They want to say no one was to blame except for the last act, which was entirely mine, but they will not. They will not undermine me. They will not threaten me. They will not—

"All done."

Startled, the glass almost slips from my grasp.

"Whoa." The beautician is there, with him at her side. "You're as jumpy as a cat. Did I just miss a firecracker going off or something?"

"No. It's nothing. I must've zoned out for a moment is all."

"Okay. So whaddaya say? He . . . she . . . polishes up real nice, don't cha think? Seems to me you could take her outside and convince anyone she's your daughter. Well, you might want to consider a different dress, something a little less . . . y'know."

She's right. My God, he is a thing of beauty. "Yeah, I'm impressed. Here, let me pay you. I'm sure you must have other appointments to get to."

"That's okay. I got time. I've shown her how to do this look so, if you like it, she should be okay with it. If you want another one, just give me a call, unless you wanna do it yourself."

She might have time. My mind is on other things.

"Oh, I'm sure we'll manage."

She continues to hustle all the way to the front door. Nice try, lady, but it's still being firmly closed behind you. Except, as she heads for the elevator, it occurs to me that now she knows my face and where I live. A mugging wouldn't be too hard to organize; fatal, of course. But then, she probably has an appointment log. The authorities will be sniffing around every name in it if she suddenly turns up dead.

By the time that's been thought through she's disappeared into the elevator, and the moment's gone. Oh well. She'll probably have forgotten by the end of the week anyway. Best to close the door and let her go.

The peace that follows is only skin-deep. My morning began with murder in mind. It isn't getting any easier. He's sitting there in the kitchen exactly as he was told to, and he looks so pretty, so desirable, so winsomely demure, a purity that must be had even if the having corrupts it. The siren's call is becoming harder and harder to resist. It would be easy enough, with the waterfront still an option once the deed is done. So what if I did? No one would know; no one but my ghosts. They've always known, waiting only for the opportunity to crowd in and bear witness to—

Stop! This is ridiculous. This is losing control. This is giving in. This needs to be dealt with once and for all with a clear head, no going back. That's it, done.

Leaving him alone should be safe enough. He's not going to screw me over, rifle through my apartment and disappear with all my valuables. He's pure innocence, like cotton candy, sweet and fluffy. Besides, he's not going anywhere dressed like that. He isn't exactly kicking up a fuss about it either, or storming out the door, so he must like it, and he probably knows he's a hell of a lot safer with it here than he would be out there on the street. It'll be fine. Really, it will.

Just to be doubly sure, instructions to clean should keep him busy. Well, that's my super-brilliant plan anyway. Not that it does anything to stop my afternoon from becoming one long wander. There are stores, cafes, and galleries to visit, but none of them interest me. Instead, the world hurries by unnoticed, all the people and the street names and time itself. A contract is nothing if not a problem to be solved, and yet here's a problem that's proving impossible. In spite of his apparent submissiveness, he's exerting some kind of influence over me. Only a fool would fail to realize that. He's been inside my head for days, too dangerous to want and yet impossible to get rid of. That's—

"Hey. Small world, huh?"

It's Joey. Like, really?

Seeing my expression, he flashes that smile at me. "Yeah, I know. I got the message. You don't work at that gallery. You're not into me."

"But you thought you'd track me down anyway."

"No, I thought I had business downtown. The rest is pure coincidence. Take a pop at me if you don't believe me."

"Yeah, right. Once is chance. Twice is coincidence. The third time someone straps you to a table and tries to cut you in half with a laser."

His hands go up in mock surrender. "Hey, what can I say? You got me. I'm just running a little late is all. My evil plan to rob Fort Knox ain't quite ready yet. I'll get back to you when I've ironed out the wrinkles. Until then, I just thought I'd stop and say hi, what with you standing there looking so lost and alone."

"I'm fine. Thanks for the concern."

"That's what friends are for, right? Oh, I'm sorry. I forgot. We ain't friends. Call me a sympathetic ear then. If you got troubles, maybe I can help."

"I'm fine. Really."

"Well, okay then." He begins to walk away, throwing at me as an afterthought, "Oh, and next time we meet—if there is a next time—I'll remember to bring my laser with me. Honestly, I'll write it down and stick it up on the fridge right next to the vault codes."

Great. That'll be something to look forward to. Another unwanted intrusion that's proving difficult to get rid of. Guys like Joey, they just don't listen. At least they can speak. The silent one is still in my apartment, a frog waiting to be kissed and probably not much of a prince to be had by way of it.

Damn him! Damn him for walking into me that day. Damn him for being there in my apartment. Damn him for being so beautiful and making me want him. My routine is shot to hell. Knowing where to be and what to do used to be so simple. Now I'm not even sure what street I'm on. God, get a grip on yourself. Throw him out. Get rid of him any which way you have to. Take back control . . . or not, because just thinking about him fills me with desire, like some cheerleader chasing a quarterback. Hell, I never even went to high school; not a normal one anyway. I'm a grown-up, professional woman. I don't have time for this. So damn him. Damn his cuteness and his prettiness and his innocence and . . . Aagh!

CHAPTER FOUR

I n the days that follow, we settle into a new routine. He will present himself properly every day, with a bra and implants under a smart uniform and proper hair and makeup. In return, he will receive free board and lodging and a safe place to sleep at night. This all seems pretty fair to me—or, at least, as fair as it's gonna be.

It works, and we become like some old married couple. Yeah, the deadliest bang in town actually just said that. Another day begins, and my hour in the gym is followed by breakfast and the news. Some guy is apologizing for comments he made years ago, with the usual mob demanding he lose his privileges. Boring!

Next stop, bargains—until something else catches my eye. A Russian oligarch's private helicopter has just mysteriously fallen out of the sky. This was some shady guy. On top of that, a known associate of his disappeared recently in New York, a nightclub owner by the name of Grigori Volkov. It might not be tied-to-a-table-and-cut-in-half-with-a-laser level but it's still one hell of a coincidence.

A trawl of the web gives me nothing more. It doesn't matter. Two and two make four and the four that's staring back at me isn't good at all, especially when cab guy is added into the equation. His last words should have been an irrelevant loose end. *"No. Wait. I can—"* Suddenly, they aren't. There's an object lesson in not acting in haste.

Doubt breeds like a contagion, and now it's two hits within weeks of each other, both with special instructions. That has me in a fever. Usually, the client wants discreet— an accident here, natural causes there. Such a shame; but then, we always thought the poor guy would work himself to death. For Grigori, someone wanted big and loud. It didn't matter who. It was just another contract. For cab guy; well, his wife was the obvious answer.

This can't be. This has to be me overthinking it. If it isn't, someone else is out there. That oligarch could be just another contract in another country. Or someone else has crunched the same numbers as me and they don't like the answer they're getting either. If so, there's only one place this is going. Loose ends are being tied up. There's a clean-up crew out there and my name just has to be on their list because anyone who knows anything is now a liability. It's an insurance policy that's kept me safely under the radar all these years.

That's it. These questions need answering, right now, and rather badly. My text joins the dots, asking if there's any reason to be concerned. Waiting for an answer is the perfect torture. This must be like wishing that hot date will call—

only he doesn't. Oh my God, just text me, will you! The growing tension even has Puppy on edge, and him standing there making out like he's my mother is just so not helping.

There's no choice. I have to get out of here, and the rest of my morning is spent walking the streets. Midday arrives, and still there's no answer. Enough of wandering the sidewalks checking my phone like a fool. An eatery will do just as well, with other patrons doing the same.

Halfway through lunch and, at last, there's a reply: someone kicked over a hornet's nest, arrangements made, pick up at central. That doesn't set my mind at ease. None of us knows who our contact is because we never meet. It's all encrypted texts and PO boxes. What if—

Calm down. Don't panic. Breathe, think, then act.

The train takes me to 31st and Penn, from where it's a short walk down 8th to the central post office: a long hall with counters on one side, doors to the street on the other, and the heraldry of dead European empires staring down from the high ceiling above. An information rack is a perfect vantage from which to pretend to browse while scanning the hall, searching for anything suspicious. The PO boxes are at the far end. It's a long walk from here to there. If this is a trap, there ain't gonna be no rubes walking into it today.

Nothing looks unusual or out of place. People are coming and going, hanging in the little seating area or waiting to be served. No one notices me pass amongst them. No one notices me watching them. They're all too busy dealing with the postal service. Not so the four standing by the boxes. Two women are holding a conversation on the street side. A couple of guys are standing apart as they loiter on the other side. One of them is very interested in his cell phone. They're all trying really hard to look ordinary, but the queen of blending in knows a fake when she sees one, and every alarm bell she's got is going off. This just has to be a setup.

The last counter before the boxes is my point of no return. Beyond that, it's game on or it's a dud. The two men are still visible to me. They are trying oh so hard, but right there is that little flick of a glance. This trap is ready to spring. All they're waiting for is those last few yards to be crossed, that box to be opened, and the ratcheting of the cuffs as they close around my wrists.

Sorry, guys, not today. This busy-busy person is late for a very important date. With a glance at my watch, I hurry for the nearest exit, with all four of them perking up like somebody just shouted "Squirrel!"

Through the exit, down the broad steps onto 8th, and straight out into the traffic on West 31st. Tires squeal. Horns blare. Someone shouts, "What the hell, lady!"

Almost at the next intersection, behind me, more tires squeal and horns blare. The pursuit is that close. Without a plan, this is going to be a very short chase.

On West 29th, cutting through some trees takes me onto West 28th, and then around onto 9th. There's a church on the corner. Just beyond is a delivery truck. Its doors are open and the delivery guy is off somewhere delivering.

Don't question it. Don't hesitate. Just crawl up inside and hide behind some boxes. Between them, there's just enough of a gap for me to watch the avenue out back.

Two of them appear. They stand on the corner, looking up and down. They've lost me. Just as the other two arrive, so does the delivery guy. The back of the truck closes. The motor starts and we move off. In the half-light and the hum, both of my phones are smashed. It's the only way to be sure phone guy hasn't hacked and tracked me.

The truck rumbles on. How far is the last thing on my mind. We stop. The back opens and delivery guy climbs in to look for a package. He's quick and doesn't see me. This time, he closes up behind him. Well, great. This is turning into a full-on mystery tour, without even a glimpse of where we are.

After a minute or so, the motor revs, and the truck moves on. Twice more this happens. There aren't that many packages left. It's a good bet delivery guy won't be too happy when he finds out about his stowaway. He'll be asking questions, maybe even calling the cops.

Fortunately, someone meets him at the next stop. They move off onto the sidewalk, too busy to notice the little mouse that jumps down from the back of the truck and crosses the street to hurry away.

This is Hell's Kitchen. It could hardly be more appropriate. On the other side of 10th is a bar. A shot of bourbon and time to think is what's needed here. The place is almost empty but still, there's some guy a couple of stools down who decides to strike up a conversation. "Hey. Must be serious to walk into a bar all on your own at this time of day."

That earns him a sour look.

"That bad, huh?"

Yeah. That bad and then some. Right now, it might not even be safe to go home. "You ever have one of those days where fate just dumps on you?"

"I'm sitting here, aren't I? So what's the deal?"

"I think the people I work for just fired me." That'll be the Network, the organization everyone like me ultimately works for—except they didn't fire me, they ratted me out.

"You think! What? You're not sure?"

He moves up to sit next to me, an average sort of guy with straggly hair, a thin beard, and well-worn clothes.

"Pretty sure. There was security and everything. You know how that works, right?"

"Jeez. You must've really pissed someone off."

The question is who. It could be the state. It could be private enterprise. They're hand in glove anyway, a deeply embedded web of influence that knows no bounds. They give us bright, shiny things to make our lives easier and, in return, we give them control over everything that used to be private. Sign up for it and you're theirs, and you better behave yourself because they don't like being messed with. Do that and they hit the button: deleted, deplatformed, canceled. And right now, they don't like me one little bit.

"Well." He orders us both another drink. "I call that as good a reason as any for hanging out in a bar. Get drunk today. Worry tomorrow. That's what I say."

"Amen to that." After my little episode the day I took Puppy home, touching that second shot is not a good idea, but what the hell. My confidence is rapidly returning. It's a warm, all-enveloping glow, like fluorescent body armor. With it comes a growing certainty. If this Deep Web knew my address, they wouldn't have gone to the trouble of setting that trap. It would have been a knock on the door and lights out.

"Okay then. Thanks for the drink but I need to make tracks."

"Nah. Stay and have another one. You got no job to rush back to, after all."

"No, but I do need to get home. Someone's waiting for me, y'know. It wouldn't look too good if I rolled up pie-eyed."

"Kid, huh?"

"Yeah. Something like that."

The door beckons. Beyond is the Deep Web, perhaps with every cop and security camera in this city in its pocket. That pretty much rules out the train, possibly buses and cabs as well. There's a long walk home in front of me. No sweat. All that's needed is a different look, a change of clothes, maybe just a different coat. It'll be fine.

There's a thrift store over on 9th. Some rummaging about comes up with a beige coat somebody must have gotten tired of real fast. A wide-brimmed fedora almost matches it, and a nylon black tote bag finishes it off. It's really quite horrible. As we small talk our way through paying for it all, the ladies at the till disagree. They want the sale, which is fair enough. Okay, it's not that bad, and here's my old coat as well. Be sure and find a good home for it. They promise they will.

Outside, my purse goes into the bag and the 9mm into my coat pocket. By now, it's late afternoon. Sunlight glints off buildings as it pours down West 43rd, making me feel all warm and glowing inside. Even the jerk-offs who pass me by with words like, "Hey, beautiful," and, "What's your number, babe?" aren't irritating me. They're mere distractions. The real crazies will be coming out when the shadows are long enough; and that's not all. Soon the streets and avenues will be filling with people heading home from work. The best way to avoid them, and any prowling cops, is to take the High Line.

It used to be an elevated railway and was saved from demolition to become a pleasant walk through the West Side, with public art and garden zones. There aren't too many people about and hurrying through it ought to be all that matters, but what the hell. Like the poet said, "What's life if you can't stop and smell the flowers?" or something like that.

The next hour or so dawdles by, a careless stroll starting at the Spur, then through the Falcone Flyover, a raised walkway through a canopy of magnolias and serviceberry.

After that is the Chelsea Thicket and a miniature forest of dogwood, holly, and roses. With the sun kissing the horizon, the little prairie of the Washington Grasslands gives way to the shade of the Gansevoort Woodland, gray birches and more serviceberry, and then the end of the line.

That's when the guy appears. He's disheveled, uncut but cleanly shaven. As we approach each other, his eyes keep flicking toward and away from me. It's hard to know if he's trying to avoid looking at me or trying to avoid being seen looking at me. Aww, poor lamb. His mom probably lectured him every day on how he's gotta respect women and now he doesn't even know how to say hello. Shyness like that is so cute until you find out you've saddled yourself with a full-on soy boy. Still, for an instant, a hug seems in order just to let him know it's okay. Nah. He might get the wrong idea. A smile will do. He gets the wrong idea anyway. Suddenly there's a grin, and his eyes are filled with cold intent.

We're yards apart. No one else is about. Almost too late, all of my alarm bells are exploding into life. Trying to avoid him is useless. The path is too narrow and he's coming straight at me with his right hand balled into a fist. My hand grips the 9mm but the damn thing is snagged on something. A smile bares super-white teeth at me. His fist opens. A knife drops into place. He lunges. My fist knocks him back a little but now he's going full psycho on me. He comes again. At last, the 9mm is free. The knife flashes. The 9mm barks until it's empty.

He's lying huddled at my feet. In the breathless moments that follow, the blade his dying hand has buried in my thigh seems unreal. It's a trick of the light or a product of my imagination. Then reality rushes in, bringing with it pain, disbelief, and outrage, like what the hell are you doing not seeing that coming, and who the hell is this punk son of a bitch asshole to think he can attack me? He deserves another mag just for the hell of it. Shame there isn't one but then there's no time for that even if there was. Everyone within half a mile must have heard those shots, and the cops won't be hobbling as they respond to all those 9-1-1 calls.

The knife pulls out easily enough and disappears into my tote. That's one DNA sample the Deep Web won't be getting today. Thankfully, no major blood vessels have been severed. There's bleeding but nothing that can't be dealt with. He's wearing some sort of scarf around his neck. It only partially stems the bleeding. His belt, looped tightly around the scarf, does the rest.

Once I'm certain there'll be no blood trail to follow, the stairs lead me down onto Gansevoort. Step by slow step, negotiating them is painful enough. Walking home is out of the question. As much of a risk as it might be, taking a cab is the only option.

East along Gansevoort and every cab sails on by. May they each be blessed with the worst fare this city can dump on their sorry asses. This is some kind of luck: giving the Deep Web the slip only to end up being skewered on the High Line, and now the damn cabs won't stop either.

At last, one pulls over. He drops me outside Bloomingdale's. It's close enough to hobble home but not so close as to step straight into a pair of cuffs. The seat of the cab is clean as the door slams on it. My bindings and coat have stopped any blood seeping onto it. That's one lead that won't be dropping into their laps.

Well into dusk by now, from the corner of Broadway and Broome, nothing seems out of the ordinary, but then it didn't at the central post office either. There are no unmarked vans or SUVs with darkened windows that have no right being here. Still, a short hobble along the south side of Broome wouldn't hurt, just to be sure.

No one jumps out to shove a badge in my face. A small army of cops doesn't suddenly appear with every gun pointed at me. SWAT, it would appear, have better things to do. Coming back on the north side, I dump the 9mm along the way. That's something that should have been done a lot sooner.

***

Inside my apartment, the stress of being hunted begins to lift. If the Deep Web knew my address, it would be here. That doesn't mean it won't be coming. If it wants me that badly, it will find me. At least there's some time to decide what to do.

That isn't the only issue that has to be dealt with. As my hat and tote are dropped to the floor, Puppy is standing there, just outside the kitchen area. He sees something is wrong but he doesn't know what it is. That look of concern irritates me because this mess should never have happened. The Deep Web's trap was all too obvious. The danger was plain and yet it was ignored. My edge has slipped. Sloppiness has opened the door to dumb mistakes. That cannot be tolerated.

My coat is thrown aside. He sees the bindings on my thigh, the dark wetness of the blood. He makes a move toward me.

"Don't! Don't you dare!"

He's confused. He doesn't understand. My anger begins to spiral. "Who the hell are you? You come out of nowhere and barge your way into my life. Why? Why me, huh? Why'd you pick on me?"

He says nothing, but that's no longer good enough. This not speaking, this innocence, it's all an act. It has to be, and he's going to be cured of it right now. He's going to give me an explanation, a simple reason, even just an excuse. "I was doing fine until you came along. I had everything under control. I was in charge of my life. Then, you appeared; you with your puppy dog eyes and your pathetic-ness. You wormed your way in, didn't you? You moved in on me like prey. Why? Did someone send you? Answer me, goddammit!"

Each word brings me closer to him, each hobbled step growing my anger into a seething rage. Still, he doesn't speak. Wrong move. This act is over. It's done. You will talk to me. A stinging slap sends him stumbling back into the kitchen. Falling to his knees, he cringes like a dog. They're all dogs, in the end, even the puppies. He looks up at me, his puppy eyes begging. That only enrages me further. Grabbing a handful of his hair, I yank his head back and fist follows fist until he's bleeding. Still he doesn't speak. Nor does he attempt to fight back. He doesn't even try to protect himself. This meekness drives me to fury. His head slams against the floor. With my thigh, kicking him is impossible. The nearest blunt instrument will do just as well. More blows rain down upon him, with me screaming all the while, "You fucking bastard! You fucking piece of shit! You ruined my life, you fucking son of a bitch . . ."

Beating and screaming, screaming and beating, it goes on until there's no longer the breath or the energy to continue. When it finally ends, he lies there curled into a ball, and tears are running down my cheeks. "You ruined my life, you bastard."

There's a knock at the door, hard and insistent, and a woman's voice calls out, "Police! Open up please!"

Shit!

She knocks again. "Are you all right in there? Open up, please, ma'am."

My mind scrambles in a moment of panic. This has to be about that asshole on the High Line. The 9mm's gone, thank God. There's still a .38 in my safe, but there isn't time to hobble to my bedroom and back. Stop. Think. This can't be about asshole because there's no way they could have identified and traced me so quickly. This could be about anything so calm down, find your Zen, deal with it.

Another knock. "Ma'am, let us know if you're okay, please."

"Yes. Hold on. I'm coming."

There are two of them beyond the door. The female officer is a little taller than me, blonde, with a concerned look on her face. Behind her stands a male officer, the muscle of the outfit.

With an intense look, she takes in the state of me. "Are you okay, ma'am? We had a report of a disturbance."

The door is only partway open with the right side of my body filling it. They can't see my wounded leg. Nor can they see Puppy curled up in the kitchen. My soaked cheeks are plain enough though. "Yes, I'm fine. Sorry about the noise."

"Are you sure?" She tries to peer past me. "The caller said it was pretty loud."

"I'm fine, really. My boyfriend . . . my ex-boyfriend . . . just dumped me by text. I lost it. I was so mad he would treat me like that, I called him up and told him exactly what I thought of him. I guess I went too far. I'm really sorry for that. It won't happen again, I promise."

"Don't worry about it. I get it, really I do. I had something like that happen to me." She leans forward for a moment, almost whispering, "Just between the two of us, I hid a brick of coke in his apartment and dropped a dime on him. He should be out in a year or two." Confidences over with, she loudly adds, "Men, huh? None of them are worth it. My advice is, have a stiff drink and go to bed."

"Yeah. Mofos!"

My pretense of smiling through the tears works. Satisfied, as she turns to leave it's her partner's turn to catch some fallout. "Come on, mofo. Night ain't over yet."

"Mofo! You best remember who's watching your back before you start throwing words like *mofo* around."

"Yeah, yeah, you've been called worse than that."

"That ain't the point. We . . ."

The door closes on their back and forth, and my pretense. My life is in ruins, wrapped around a tree like some guy's midlife crisis fresh off the forecourt. With my back against the wall, there's nothing to do but sink to the floor, curl up, and cry myself to sleep.

CHAPTER FIVE

Morning comes, and my bed is warm and cozy. That only lasts a moment because my leg hurts like hell. I throw back the covers to find my thigh cleaned and bandaged, and all of yesterday's events rush back in on me. They hurt just as much. Every careful step, every act of denial and control, all of it floats around me like wreckage on a reef. There are no routines to deal with this, no smart plans or ready stories. There is only desolation, an ocean fit for drowning in.

Sunlight glints as it pours in through the windows, but it cannot lift me. All those offshore accounts beyond the Deep Web's reach cannot lift me. If only my bed would open up and swallow me whole like in some cheesy horror flick. Even the ridiculousness of that thought cannot lift me.

Quietly he enters the room. He's made breakfast. Mother Teresa he ain't, yet here he is, making out like he's some kind of saint, and that must include the dressing on my thigh. "Did you do this?"

He nods. It's pure innocence, without a hint of judgment or reproach, unlike the bruises on his face. Those are my doing, the marks of my rage unleashed, and that is even more crushing.

"Oh, baby." At my beckoning, the tray is set aside and he comes to sit beside me. "I'm so sorry. I don't know what came over me."

He smiles, not even flinching at the touch of my hands. There's just a hug and, for a moment, we hold each other. "Baby, I promise. I promise this will never happen again."

Tears start to flow, but this time they are tender and filled with remorse. To deliberately choose to hurt something so beautiful, so gentle, is unforgivable, and yet, as we hold each other, there is nothing but forgiveness, and it deserves a name. "You're my angel, my Angie. That's what I'm going to call you from now on. My Angie. My dear, sweet Angie."

Pulling away, he points at himself and mouths *Angie*. Then he points at me, his eyes forming the unspoken question.

"Beth. My name is Beth."

Suddenly, everything has changed. He can never be my toy again. Naming him has made him human. In giving him my name, something of me has been let loose too. The feeling is as certain as the pain in my leg, even if its name is unknown. We hug again as though meeting for the first time, and my despair begins to recede. He has lifted me, at least to the point where it's possible to begin dealing with this disaster.

"Come on. Those cops last night, they might come back." Not to mention the Deep Web, who've now had half a day to hunt me down. "We have to get out of here. First of all, though, we're going to have to hide those bruises."

***

He sits at my vanity. A good smothering of foundation hides the telltale marks of my rage well enough. Then the maid's uniform is replaced with a full skirt and boots, floral blouse, and full-skirted coat. A chiffon scarf hides his Adam's apple. The boots are tight— his feet are larger than mine—but we'll have to deal with that later. For me, dark pants and a thin turtleneck will do.

Next, two suitcases are packed. There are enough clothes to get by, but then we can always buy more if we need them. More importantly, there are several wigs and a full makeup kit. My well-stocked first aid kit comes too because this thigh of mine is sure as hell not going anywhere near a hospital.

Also, there are the contents of my safe. Inside are multiple fake IDs, all of them for me. There simply isn't time to get any for him. There's the .38 as well, with two magazines, and ten thousand dollars. The gun slips quietly into my purse. He doesn't need to know about that. Finally, with me wearing a dark-brown coat, we're good to go until we're almost out the door. My laptop. The Deep Web doesn't need to find that when it finally raids this place.

Down on Broome, we pause in the doorway. Still no suspect vans or SUVs. Side by side we walk to Broadway with our suitcases trundling behind us. My leg is bearable. No one notices anything suspicious. We're just two girls starting out on a journey. Hell, some smartass even eyeballs my Angie like he's got a chance. With me eyeballing him back, he gets the message and goes on about his day.

On Broadway, a cab is surprisingly easy. The driver knows a cheap hotel, the kind where they rent by the hour and ask no questions. When he drops us off, we wait until he's gone, then walk to another hotel. If he turns us in, the Deep Web can knock itself out raiding the wrong joint. Besides, one fleapit is much the same as another, and this second hotel is about as five-star as a dumpster. The only service is some grubby, sullen guy sitting at the end of a narrow, dingy lobby. Its dark walls are lined with faded posters under struggling lighting. Beneath is threadbare carpeting and fraying couches that might be hotels for something else. From inside a cubicle behind wire mesh he watches us approach, weighing up the fatness of our pocketbook. That'll be the rent doubled, right there. Never mind. We came for the privacy, not the ambiance.

"How much for a week for two?"

He looks at me. He looks at Angie. "You two . . . together?"

Yeah, us two . . . together. And don't think that hot lesbian sex fantasy playing out behind your eyes hasn't been noticed either.

"You see anyone else? And you can take that look off your face as well. Not that it's any of your business but she's my daughter, so check it. Now you got a room or not? And I better not find any nasty little holes or cameras in there either."

With barely a change in his expression, he quotes a price. It's daylight robbery for sure, but I pay him extra on top anyway. "We don't want to be disturbed, understand? By anybody."

He shrugs. His horny little mind has other things to think about.

Our room is just as bad as the lobby: tired, shabby, and filled with the spore of previous occupants. There's nothing quite so welcoming as strange hairs in the sink. Ugh! Whatever they spend the rent on here, it sure ain't room service. That's okay. With any luck, my junked laptop won't be found until the building is demolished. It's also quiet—most of the time—and it has a TV that works. Throughout the days that follow, it stays firmly on the news. In the evenings, Angie gets to watch what he wants. It's usually pretty awful, but that's the price of waiting for my thigh to heal.

Two days later, the Deep Web goes public with asshole on the High Line. There's a grainy image of me lifted from some CCTV. It's a close-up, real close-up, but an observant eye can still make out the lower parts of a cycling helmet. Crap! Cab guy's mistress did have recording equipment. Now they have my face; they know exactly who dropped the hammer. From that, they must've tracked down every one of my hotels. Phone records would have done the rest, leading them straight to my contact and, oh man, would you look at this. An entire network of murder for hire they never even knew existed. The back-slapping must've been heard for miles.

They don't care about asshole. He's just a convenient cover to plaster me all over the news. Never mind. The only person who knows we're here is the guy downstairs, and he doesn't strike me as the kind who even watches the news. Hell, he's probably still high on imagining what we're doing up here. We should be safe enough.

For the rest of our time here Angie gets a crash course in how to walk and behave because it takes more than fake tits and a dress to turn a boy into a girl.

Five days later, Angie returns from a food run in a fluster. She's confident enough to go out on her own now. It's sort of a weird thing to have to confess but it's becoming really hard to remember she's a boy. The cause of her concern she tries to convey to me by pointing at the floor. Something has happened in the lobby but, despite all of her gesticulating, it's impossible to understand what. She finds a pen and paper and begins to write. Funny; it never once occurred to me to ask whether she could read and write. When she hands it to me, it's a childish scrawl but it's easy enough to read. *There are men in the lobby asking questions.*

"What men?"

Don't know. Not cops.

"What did the guy in the cage tell them?"

Don't know. Nothing, I think. He saw me watching.

"Pack, now. We're leaving."

As we creep down to the lobby, we're both dolled up: short skirts, big wigs, and enough makeup to decorate a small apartment. For a pair of hookers sneaking out with our john's valuables, we just about pass muster. Not that there's anyone to see. Whoever the men asking questions were, they're long gone. Grubby guy isn't in his cage either. He's round the corner somewhere arguing with someone. There are a couple of other guys standing by: old, down-and-out, the kind who hang around for the warmth and company until they're told to scram. Right now, with their backs to us, they're too busy enjoying the entertainment.

We disappear out onto the street and hail a cab. Midtown, we dump it and hail another. Three cab rides later and we're in the suburbs, outside a storage garage, an accommodation address for one of my PO boxes. The only thing inside is a tarp. Underneath is a two-door, soft-top Jeep. It's properly registered and plated and purrs every time it's taken out for some exercise. We sleep in it, not very comfortably, the daylight hours in between filled off and on with me trying to find out who Angie is.

"Where did you come from?"

She names some little town in upstate New York. It's most likely the first place to pop into her head.

"So who are your parents? Where are they?"

She doesn't know. She's just another lost child, all alone in the world—except for me.

"But the state must have taken care of you. Didn't they send you to a home or something?"

She doesn't remember, or she won't say. That's not exactly a surprise. Foster homes are no mystery to me. "Don't worry, sweetie. You're with me now. We're going to stick together and see the world, just you and me, without any child services or police or anyone else to tell us what to do."

She smiles at that, reaching out to take me in her arms. A warm glow fills me, strangely comforting, like drinking hot soup on a cold winter's night. A gale might be rattling the windows but we are wrapped up warm in front of a roaring fire, snug and protected, because that's what this is all about: being protected. From now on, she will be. Wherever we end up and however we get there, she will be safe because she is mine and no one is going to harm her without going through me.

For the next few days, my thigh continues to heal until it's fit enough for me to drive. My attempts to coax more information out of her are not so rewarding. She is easily as stubborn as me, unless it's a trust thing. Well, trust takes time, and it works both ways. Push her too hard and she might start asking *me* questions. That's a bridge that's not going to be crossed until it absolutely has to be, if ever.

Besides, for now, it's the Hudson we need to be crossing. Wherever that knife had been before asshole stuck me with it, the blade must have been clean because there's been no infection. The beautician has probably given up my apartment by now. If the men asking questions came back, the hotel guy has probably given us up too. As for everyone else, the news cycle waits for no one. They're all sitting there in front of their TVs watching the next fleeting outrage by now. So long as we keep our heads down, we'll be free and clear. It's time to leave.

The suitcases are thrown in the back of the Jeep. Angie helps me open the garage doors and we look out onto a bright, sunny day. Maybe it's a good omen.

***

We're heading west. Perhaps we ought to be heading north into Canada, but anything that keeps the Deep Web guessing is fine by me. North or south, Canada or Mexico; both borders are largely open. We could cross almost anywhere unseen. Or perhaps that's a decision that's being avoided because here we are, two girls on a road trip with the top down, our hair blowing in the wind and hard rock pumping from the radio. One of us is singing along, loud and hard, and wishing the other one could too. Perhaps she could write along in capitals. Nah. That's just silly. Not that there's anything wrong with silliness. Silliness is what helps make life fun, and the noisy one here is having way too much fun to worry about all that other stuff.

We stop for lunch in Allentown, eating at a table out on the sidewalk. As we sit, a cruiser rolls by. Neither of the cops inside pays us any mind. There's no reason why they should. We're just two more faces in the crowd, a mother and daughter spending some quality time together.

After we've eaten, we visit the Liberty Bell Museum next door. Angie isn't really that interested, but it doesn't take too long. On the way out, our cover is unexpectedly tested. We run into a lady. As homey as apple pie and as sturdy as a shotgun, she is also polite to a fault, and we find ourselves caught in one of those "You first," "No, you first," situations. Once we're out on the sidewalk, she casts an appraising eye over Angie. "Is this your daughter?"

"Why, yes. She is."

"And so pretty too. You could even be sisters, the pair of you."

Some guy on the street in New York would probably have ogled anything in a dress. This lady is up close and personal, and she's buying it. My delight at that comes out all momsy pleased. "Thank you. It's so kind of you to say so."

She turns back to Angie. "And how about you, sweetheart? Did you enjoy visiting our museum?"

"Oh, I'm afraid she can't speak. It's a birth defect, you know."

Why Angie is mute is something she still refuses to be drawn on. It has to be some kind of trauma hiding away inside her. Until it can be coaxed out of her, a birth defect is as good a story as any.

"Oh, that's such a pity. But I'm sure if you could, your voice would be just as beautiful as you are."

Angie plays along, smiling sweetly.

"Yes, it's a pity, but still, she's my little gift from God."

"Well aren't they all? And that reminds me. I have two sons myself. I swear they never stop eating, God bless the pair of them. I must be getting along. Well, enjoy the rest of your stay in our little town."

As she hurries away, Angie reaches into her purse for a notepad and pen and writes: *you're my mom?*

"Why not? Wouldn't you like me to be your mom?"

But it's a lie.

"We have to tell these people something, sweetie, and sometimes a lie is a good thing."

She thinks about that for a moment, her brow faintly furrowing as she tries to figure it out. That is just so huggable, except Mommy is trying to get ahead of whatever answer she's coming back with. When it arrives, it's the last thing Mommy wants to be dealing with.

Is that why you lied to the police?

Suddenly, hugs are at the back of the line. At the front is a convincing explanation for what happened the day the Deep Web nearly caught me, and the truth can't be any more of it than can be gotten away with. Trust works both ways, and hers is as important to me as her innocence. Mommy's little secret might destroy both.

"Yes. I was protecting us. Didn't I tell you that? I met a bad man. He attacked me. I think I hurt him more than he hurt me. If the police find us, they might arrest me. They might take you away. They might send you back to where you came from. You don't want that, do you?"

Her eyes lock gaze with mine, her brow almost furrowing again. Whatever she's thinking, my only hope is that she'll let it go. Please, baby, believe me. You don't need to know anymore. You only need to trust me. This time, when her answer comes, it's a simple: *no.*

My arm slides around her waist and pulls her close. "I know. It's hard but, really, I'm only trying to keep us safe, to keep us together. Once we're out of all of this, no one will ever be able to hurt us again. You do believe me, don't you?"

She smiles and nods. This squall has been averted. Mommy can breathe again.

"Good. Let's hit the road then. We can make Harrisburg before nightfall."

CHAPTER SIX

A ngie can't drive. Maybe she ran away before anyone could teach her. That's something that will have to be taken care of. As the only driver, when we reach Harrisburg in the late afternoon, all day behind the wheel has me fit to drop. This road trip of ours will go a lot more easily if she can bear some of the burden. Anyway, we're here now, and we find a hotel one street over from the Susquehanna.

This is going to be our first night on the road together, so we're going to celebrate. For an hour, we rest up, then freshen up and dress up. Angie is in a slim, red dress with a gold chain and, damn, does she wear it well. Some little, petal-shaped studs would complete her perfectly, except she doesn't have pierced ears. Adding that to the to-do list, for me there's a black, knee-length dress with a fuller skirt, plain but brightened up a little with a brooch of blue glass set in silver and a chunky necklace. One last look before we head out and it's hang on to your hats, Harrisburg, because we are one hot pair of babes. Well, one hot mother-daughter combo, anyway. That may be something Mommy's going to have to force herself to remember, in public at least.

Minutes later, our cab drops us outside a tavern. The driver swears it serves the best wings in town. It's just a touch olde-worlde with its white walls and old wood, its rustic chairs and its big stone fireplace with a clock in the middle. It's also busy, and we stand by the bar sipping cocktails while we wait for a table.

As we mind our own business, with me fussing over Angie's hair and jewelry, there are a lot of glances coming our way. The men are all like, yeah. Their partners are all like, remember who you're here with, sweetheart, or you'll be sleeping on the couch tonight. At the other end of the bar though, there are two men with no such restraints. A pair of corn-fed cocks on the prowl, they might both of them be irresistible in uniform. At last deciding to try their luck, they begin to work their way toward us. As they come close, it's not what kind of company we're in for that has me thinking. It's which one of them has chosen to hit on Angie, because this definitely ain't gonna be your night, fella.

The first smiles broadly as they arrive. "Hey. Haven't seen you here before. So are you new to Harrisburg or just this place?"

"Hey. Yeah, we just got in. Me and my daughter decided to take ourselves off on a road trip, y'know?"

"A road trip, huh? Wow, that's quite an adventure. Always sort of thought I'd like to do that myself but somehow, something always seems to get in the way. An old buddy's getting married. Your sister's having a christening.

Your mom wants to know when you're going to give her a grandchild. Before you know it, BAM, there's another year gone by. So how long are you staying over for?"

"Just the one night. We have a long way to go, like, clear across the country. Sometimes you just gotta say to hell with it, we're going, and so, here we are."

"Well yeah, I guess so." He looks at Angie. He's expecting her to say something but the birth defect story soon takes care of that. He seems quite sympathetic. His friend is another matter. Until now, he's done nothing but stand there and grin like a fool. Now he proves it by saying, "Wow! I guess deep throat is out then."

We all look at him, the expression on his friend's face saying it all. *You're supposed to be my wingman, not a goddam kamikaze.*

"What?" Funny guy doesn't get it, the poor, misunderstood little lamb. "It was a joke!"

"A joke!" Never mess with a mother and her daughter. "You wanna deep throat my little girl and you think it's a joke? How about I get a strap on and deep throat you, huh? Would you think that was funny?"

While Angie stands beside me looking all innocent because she's a good girl who doesn't understand any of this, funny guy goes all Chernobyl, right there in the middle of the restaurant. "Ah, screw you, lady! I wouldn't touch your precious little brat if you paid me to. I wouldn't touch you either, bitch!"

He stalks off, barging his way through the now silent and staring restaurant. Oh well, never mind. It's not as if there was going to be any hooking up here anyway. In spite of that, there's still just a tiny hint of sympathy for his friend. "Yeah. I'm sorry about that. He just went through a bad breakup, y'know. It's always been everything or to-hell-with-you with him, even way back in high school. Good on the sports field, not so good off it. I guess I better go calm him down. Enjoy the rest of your evening."

He's a nice guy, so he can safely be forgotten as soon as his back is turned. Funny guy is forgotten too. He's nice guy's problem. Besides, with the restaurant returning to normal, our table is ready.

We sit opposite each other, and our order of wings, sweet potato fries, and beer arrives in good time. The beer is cold, the wings are hot, and we giggle together as we get all messy eating them. After that, we walk out to the Susquehanna and find a sunken garden. Holding hands, we cross North Front Street and stroll between the little hedges and around the gazebo. From there it's down to the river bank and we wander our way back to the hotel, arm in arm as we take in the evening air. There is nothing to say. Words would simply ruin such a perfect silence, which is something else funny guy apparently doesn't get.

"Hey!"

We face him, one of us with more than just a little exasperation. Nice guy said he would calm him down but he must have gotten away and that's a deep, deep bottle he's been drowning his sorrows in. Also, he's been following us, and that ain't to my liking at all.

Stumbling toward us, he tries to snarl through the booze. "So what is it with you two, huh? Yeah, I see you. I see you acting all like mother and daughter. You think you got everybody fooled, don't cha. Well, not me! I see you holding hands and all, making out like a man ain't good enough for you. So what are you then, a pair of dykes or something?"

Here we go again, only this time, it ain't some grubby guy in a fleapit hotel having a wet dream. This time it's a drunk who could be dangerous, although that doesn't stop me thinking *Oh, honey, if you only knew the truth.*

Moment over. Now to deal with it. If you want dykes, baby, you got dykes. Be careful what you wish for though because it's not uncommon for one of them to be a bull and you've just become a red rag.

My curves begin to sway, oozing sultriness as they work their way toward him. "Oh, baby, I'm sorry. We didn't mean to hurt your feelings. Come on now. Let me make it up to you."

Poor darling. He stands there like a big, dumb deer, unable to drag his eyes off my headlights even as I raise my hands to cup his face. "Baby, we can still be friends. If that's what you want."

Before he can even begin to respond, his face collapses into a grimace of pain. Yeah, that'll be my knee in your nuts. He crumples, collapsing into a poor, moaning heap at my feet. From there, he looks up at me like where did that express train just come from? The poor lamb. He's in need of some TLC. What he gets as he watches me crouch down in front of him is, "Aww, baby, I'm sorry. I guess I must've just plain forgotten what a man keeps between his legs, what with me being a dyke and all. How about this? You stop following us, and I won't show you any of the other places it really, really hurts. That sound good to you?"

Beyond the tears, he has nothing to say for himself.

"I'll take that as yes then, shall I? Great. So you be a good boy now and run along home, or should I say crawl. Either way, I'm sure you'll be as good as new in a day or two. And if anyone asks, you can just tell them you're saddle sore or something."

Now he's drooling like a hound. That's somewhat disgusting, but also just a little bit satisfying. Whatever he thought he was gonna do, he ain't doing it now. That feeling is short-lived though because there's Angie waiting for me, and she's not looking pleased at all. In fact, she's horrified. The first violence she saw from me was the beating she took in my apartment. Now she's seen me beat on someone else. This is not good, and it'll be even worse if someone else comes by.

"Come on, baby. We'd best get back to the hotel."

She is resistant, accusatory even, pulling back from my hand with enough strength so that, without more violence, she can't be forced.

"Look! That guy was going to attack us. You do understand that, don't you? We had to leave New York because of a jerk like him. Do you want to stand around here and wait for the cops to turn up? Do you want them to identify us and likely send us back? Is that what you want to happen?"

No, she doesn't. With her resistance turning to sullen compliance, we hurry back to our room. Once the door is closed behind us, she stands across from me, holding me in a cold gaze. It's all the eloquence she needs.

"I had to, baby. You know I had to. He was going to attack us."

Her gaze is unchanging. This would be so much easier if she could talk but, right now, she doesn't seem to want to write anything either. Even when her notepad and pen are thrust at her, she will not offer me anything that might give me an in. "Please. Tell me you understand. I'm not like that. I don't hurt people because I enjoy it. Even when I hurt you, it wasn't because I wanted to. I was angry. I'd just been stabbed in the leg, for chrissakes. You do understand that, don't you?"

She refuses. My God, Angie, write something. It was me who took you off the streets. It was me who put a roof over your head and . . . maybe that's what this is really all about. Close enough to reach out to her, this time, she doesn't back away.

"You want me to apologize again? You want me to say sorry for the way I treated you? I wanted you from the first moment I saw you. I don't know why, and I don't know why I humiliated you like that. Maybe it was because I wanted you. Maybe it was because I just didn't know any other way to behave. You're the only one I've ever let in. You're the only one I've ever allowed to come close to me. Maybe that was just too much for me. Maybe I just couldn't handle it and, baby, I'm sorry for that, truly I am. But I promised I would never hurt you again. I meant that. And I won't let anyone else hurt you either. God alone knows what that jerk might have done—"

Suddenly, she raises a hand and presses her fingers against my lips. The coldness is gone from her eyes. In its place is something else: acceptance, perhaps. Whatever it is, it brings with it a wave of relief.

"Oh, Angie. I only ever wanted us to be together. All the rest of it is just—"

She leans in and kisses me. It's so unexpected that, for an instant, my whole being freezes. Ah, what the hell. She's been off-limits for long enough. Besides, there's nearly twenty years of denial just aching to be caught up on. We come together, growing ever more passionate as all restraint is thrown to the wind. Hands run over faces and through hair. Zips and clasps are fumbled at; clothes discarded who knows where until we are naked on the floor. Wanting him now, needing him now, the rest of this night is lost in the heat of our desire.

★★★

CHAPTER SIX

Next morning, we leave Harrisburg early. It's best, all things considered. Funny guy is unlikely to be filing a complaint because what man would? Please, Officer, a woman half my size in heels just crushed my nuts. Get outta here, you pussy! There are also the guests in the neighboring rooms to consider. Who knows how many of them might have lain awake all night, listening. Who knows how many of them might start comparing notes over breakfast. In that room! A mother and her daughter! Are you sure? Oh my God, what was that? On both counts, we're not waiting around to find out.

A little over half an hour later, we're across the Susquehanna and pulling into Carlisle. There we stop for breakfast, except Angie isn't eating anything. She's decided to come over all playful: pouting, squirming, giggling, and brazenly flirting. This has to be because of last night. Then she threatens to start flicking food at me.

"Don't you dare! Behave yourself!"

She picks up a menu and hides the lower half of her face behind it. Above it, her eyes grin wickedly.

"Stop it! You're gonna have everyone looking at us. Now eat something or you'll go hungry 'til lunch."

"I know." The waitress stops by to refill my coffee. "I got one just the same. They're hell at that age."

"Tell me about it. And she used to be so sweet as well."

"Honey, you just wait 'til the boys come calling. You'll think teething was a walk in the park."

She wanders off to serve another customer. Well, at least that's one thing this mom doesn't have to worry about. The boys aren't ever going to come calling—not unless they want a nasty surprise. And that, right now, is the problem. This is turning out to be something of a nasty surprise for me. This boy has been taught to move like a girl, behave like a girl, and seek attention like a girl. She is becoming a monster, and that sap Frankenstein thought he had it tough.

"For God's sake! We're supposed to be mother and daughter. Now stop flirting and behave like it."

It doesn't help that part of me is actually quite enjoying this, and she almost certainly knows it. She has learned far too quickly the power of her own prettiness, what with those tumbling, highlighted curls framing her adorably coquettish face. If she doesn't start behaving herself, something will have to be done, although quite what has me stumped. Taking out a mob boss or a corrupt politician: easy. This—not so much.

After breakfast, we go shopping. The weather is growing warmer and there is only a limited wardrobe in our suitcases. First of all, there are two summer dresses, one with a large floral design and the other white with little embroidered flowers. Two big, floppy straw hats and a pair of shawls will finish them nicely. We'll wear them later. After that, a pair of boots for her before she starts hobbling around like she's breaking in a new pair of stilettos. Finally, we have her ears pierced and buy her some studs. She's very brave about it.

From Carlisle, we go out into the backwoods. The roads are well-made, with dense trees on both sides and few other vehicles about. It's the perfect place to put a novice behind the wheel.

Once we've pulled over, the whole thing starts to look a little different. Putting my life and my Jeep in her hands may be about as stupid as it gets. That gaze she's giving me isn't helping either, what with its winning smile positively dripping with innocence and charm, all of it saying it'll be fine, really.

"All right, babe. Swap over."

She beams at that, running around the Jeep as we exchange seats. At least there's no shortage of enthusiasm. Now let's see what happens once she's started it up.

"Slowly, okay. We've got the road to ourselves and all morning to do this. So gently on the gas until you start to get a feel for it."

The grin she gives me in reply is simply angelic. Sure enough, we start to move off nice and easy. Then she looks at me again and her eyes turn into pure demon spawn. Her foot goes down hard on the gas, the tires screech, and suddenly we're hurtling earthward without a parachute. Thankfully, the road ahead is still empty. It's the trees on either side that aren't so safe. The hand brake bites, slowing us to an angry halt. "What the hell! You've barely even sat behind the wheel for the first time and you think this is NASCAR or something!"

The demon within her turns defiant. Seizing her purse, she takes out her notepad and writes: *Oh my God, you're so controlling!*

Well, at least her writing is improving.

"Controlling! You're damn right I'm controlling. If it wasn't for me, you'd still be living on the streets. Is that what you want?"

She isn't listening. She's writing. The note she hands me says: *I'm not a kid, you know. I can look after myself.*

"Oh really. Out here, all on your own, miles from anywhere with no money, no transport, and it gets really dark at night. You think you can handle that, do you, without me to protect you?"

She gets out of the Jeep, slams the door, and walks a few yards down the highway. There she stands, arms folded, and pouting. Of course, she's challenging me, testing boundaries. Maybe she's even trying to establish some kind of superiority. Who knew one night of rampant sex could bring about such a change? Well, it ain't gonna fly, sweetie. As pretty as your butterfly wings might be, you ain't in charge around here. Not that walking up to her and saying that is an option. She's being quite bone-headed enough. No. This is a moment for approaching softly, for giving a little and biding my time.

"I'm sorry, baby. I shouldn't have snapped at you like that. Why don't we forget it ever happened? It would be silly to fall out over something so small. Now please, get back in the Jeep. We still have a way to go before nightfall."

She writes a note. It says: *No.*

"Sweetheart, I—"

She turns on me, pushes me away and walks a little farther along the highway. Forced to take a step backward, my surprise quickly turns to anger. Pushing boundaries is one thing. Pushing me is quite another. That, sweetie, is not going to be stood for.

"Enough of this! I don't know what's gotten into you but you need to remember who's paying for everything around here. Your clothes, your food, your transport, and the bed you sleep in at night. You will—"

Mouthing something decidedly unladylike in my face, she stalks off some more. Well, to hell with this.

"Fine! Enjoy the nightlife, young lady, because it's certainly going to enjoy you!"

Back at the Jeep, I slam the door and screech the tires, leaving her standing in the dust. You little bitch. Let's see how long you survive without me. Let's see you try to fool the world without me there to back you up. Let's see you try to twist an actual man around your little finger, especially if he tries to take advantage and finds out what's really between your legs. Good luck with all of that, sweetheart, because from now on, you're on your own.

CHAPTER SEVEN

The highway stretches out before me, free and clear, and the gas is right there beneath my foot, but still she's holding me back. And she's got me talking to myself.

"What is it with her?"

There's no one to hear me but the trees, standing like silent judges robed in green.

"I mean it. Seriously. What is it with her? I never lose my temper but here she is driving me nuts."

The gas is right there. Just a little more pressure; that's all it needs.

"I'm doing it. I swear I am."

The trees don't believe me. They're not the only ones. Whatever the cord connecting us, it will not break. My hands grip the wheel hard. My head is pressed back against the headrest. The sky doesn't believe me either.

"Aaagh! How is she doing this to me? And don't tell me it's love. I don't do love. Love is . . . I don't know what it is, but that thing in Harrisburg, that was lust, nothing more, just plain, old lust. I mean, my God. Me: in love. How ridiculous is that?"

It doesn't matter how ridiculous it is because the trees aren't buying it. If they had faces they'd be grinning. If they had voices, they'd be saying, "Yeah, right." As for the sky, well, it's just sitting up there looking as smug as hell.

"Okay, you win! But I swear if this gets any messier, well, I don't know. That's all I'm saying."

Back along the highway and, oh crap, Angie isn't alone. There's a man with her, and he's state police: right here, right now, in the middle of this forest. We are barely a day out of New York. The Deep Web can't have caught up to us that fast; even if the beautician turned me in, even if the guy in the flea pit hotel turned us in, even if someone in Harrisburg filed a complaint.

Just play it cool, see where it goes.

The .38 slips into my right coat pocket and my current fake ID into the left. The trooper's been trying to question Angie but he's getting no answers. Probably already bugged at that, he's in no mood to be dealing with someone turning up out of nowhere and just deciding to butt in. "Ma'am. Unless you know this girl, I'm going to have to ask you to drive on."

"I do. I'm her mother."

"You have some ID?" He's stone-faced. Either he doesn't believe me or he doesn't think much of my parenting skills. Only someone with kids of their own is that judgmental.

My IDs are all good; the best a great deal of money can buy. While he inspects this one, my attention turns to Angie. The way she's standing says it all. Arms folded tightly across her chest and eyes glued to the ground, she wishes she was anywhere but here. Good. Let this be a lesson you don't forget any time soon, young lady.

"Thank you." He hands my ID back to me. "So, you're her mother, are you? Can you prove that?"

"Yes. You've been questioning her, right? Well, the reason she's not answering is she can't talk. She can write, though. Give her your notebook. She'll tell you."

She'd better or this is going to turn real bad, real fast. He thinks about it. Both my hands are back in my pockets, with Mommy looking just the right amount of sorry because she knows she did a bad thing. Mommy's fingers are still curled around the grip of the .38 though, just in case.

He decides, handing Angie his notebook but keeping an eye firmly on me. "Write down your name and date of birth, sweetheart. Mommy should know those, don't you think?"

Oh, crap! Angie looks at me but she's on her own with this one. She's seen my current ID. She knows the name. She has to get this right. Taking the notebook, she begins to write. My thumb is on the safety.

With the notebook back in his hands, he takes his time reading what she's written. "Okay. What's her full name?"

"Angel Kerswick. Her name's Angel Kerswick."

He nods. "And her date of birth?"

Here goes nothing. Fifteen sounds about right, but this time, he doesn't nod. That's no big surprise.

"Not what she's written here," He's eyeing me all over again, like my parenting skills just hit rock-bottom.

Absolutely he's a parent, and one of them is almost certainly a girl.

"Yeah well, you know how it is. They're always lying about their age, trying to get into bars and stuff. You tell them not to, you ground them for weeks but still they go right ahead and do it. You got daughters yourself, right? Boys are so much easier. They misbehave, you make them take out the trash for a week. But girls . . ."

He's wavering. It's right there in the flicking of his pen, like the tail of a cat that hasn't quite decided yet whether or not to rake its claws across the back of your hand.

"Look, I'm really sorry. It was just a silly fight; y'know, a mother and daughter thing. I never intended to abandon her. I just wanted to give her some time to think it over. It was stupid of me and I swear it won't happen again."

He flicks his pen a few more times. This is a dilemma for both of us, and it could still go either way. He has a duty to perform, but he's also a parent himself. My thumb is still on the safety, just waiting for the word.

His pen stops flicking and the word is . . . Mommy isn't getting off without a slapped wrist. "You do realize, don't you, ma'am, that I could take you in for this. You'd be facing a charge of abandonment and your daughter would end up in child services. You don't want that to happen, do you?"

"No, I don't. Honestly, it won't happen again, as God is my witness."

"Well, you don't look like the kind to willfully dump a kid. Believe me, I know; but take this as a timely warning anyway. The next officer who finds her standing all alone by the side of the road might not be so generous. And as for you, young lady. Stop lying about your age. It's not clever, and it's not funny."

"Thank you, Officer. Maybe she'll listen to you."

His expression as he turns to leave says he doubts it. Yeah, he's got a daughter for sure. He knows the score. As he pulls away, my daughter is back to standing with her eyes firmly on the ground. So she should. She's embarrassed me in front of that nice officer and she ought to be made to say sorry. She ought to be grounded for a month, and then some. Except now she's looking so sorry and lost and pitiful that Mommy simply doesn't have the heart for it. You poor little thing. A big hug and kiss it all better is what's needed here, if it wasn't for a state trooper who might right now be headed back to his station and a wanted notice for a murder in New York.

"Come on, baby, back in the Jeep."

***

We stop for the night in Morgantown. It's a good place to disappear amongst the crowd of students from West Virginia University. We've had a good drive. Well, one of us has. Angie has been pretty quiet, but that's a good thing. Her quietness means more attentiveness so that her driving is improving rapidly. What else might be going on inside her pretty head, only time will tell.

After finding a hotel, we cross over to an Irish bar in search of something to eat. It's low-key, with reasonable food, inexpensive drinks, and a friendly crowd. It doesn't take long for us to fall in with a group at the next table. There are four of them and they introduce themselves as Matt and Abby and Jeff and Caitlin. They're all medical students. We're Dana and Annie and we're traveling across the country together. The rest they make up for themselves and, since they're not entirely wrong, that suits me fine.

"Wow." Abby is a tumble of brown curls that frame her round face. She has a no-nonsense attitude that must come from cutting up dead people. Maybe a certain someone even supplied one or two of them. "So how long have you guys been together?"

"Oh, just a little while. We sort of met in the street and just hit it off immediately."

"Even though she can't speak." Matt is lean, a clean-cut blond with piercing eyes that betray a quick mind. He could probably be a rock legend if he wanted to, but he'll likely end up a brain surgeon. He'll be a millionaire either way.

"Well, yeah. That was part of the attraction. I just looked into her eyes and BAM, there I was, gone."

"I think that's just awesome." With her mix of earnestness and empathy, Caitlin already has the perfect bedside manner. As warm as she is plump, and with deep, dark eyes, she has a career in terminal care waiting for her. "And you look so happy together."

Angie's hand is in mine. We squeeze together. Jeff says nothing. He's sitting there with his broad shoulders hunched forward as he watches and listens with the intensity of an eagle. He's got shrink written all over him, and that makes him someone to keep an eye on.

Meanwhile, Caitlin is cooing. "Aww, it's so sweet. You're just made for each other."

"You fancy some girl action then, do you?" That earns Matt a dig in the ribs from Abby. "Oh my God, don't be such a douche. It's not always about men you know."

"I never said it was. Jeez, you can't even make a joke anymore without someone getting offended." Matt drops out of the conversation, looking pretty offended himself, but no one cares. Abby and Caitlin are more interested in us, and so is Jeff, who continues to watch in silence, his own dark eyes just taking it all in.

"So," says Abby to me while Caitlin engages with Angie, "how far have you come?"

"Providence. Yeah, we thought we'd head over to California, maybe catch some waves."

Angie's hand slips from mine. She begins to write Caitlin a note. That could turn into a mess real fast. Tempting as it is to sneak a read before it's handed over, Abby is turning all misty-eyed. "Oh, I know. All those surfer dudes, right? I'm sorry. You're probably not interested in that. Truth is, half of them are smacked out of their heads anyway. You know, 'just waitin' to catch a wave, bro,' that sort of thing."

"Well, maybe we'll find some surfer chicks instead. Or are they all smacked out of their heads too?"

Abby gives a little shrug. "Who can tell? Maybe they're just Valley girls. Oh my God, y'know, like, totally. No, seriously. I shouldn't make fun of people like that. I'm sorry."

"Because that would be valleyist, or something like that?"

Abby laughs behind her hand with a little shake of her head that suggests she knows she shouldn't but she can't stop herself. My innocent smile plays along because this game is just too easy. Feed her the right lines and she just keeps apologizing.

Meanwhile, Caitlin and Angie are getting along like BFFs, all smiles and confidences. Whatever Angie's writing, she must also be coming up with the right lines. Well they do say a good teacher can change lives.

Whether or not she's convincing Jeff is another matter. Still observing everything with that eagle eye, he's now also reading her discarded notes. As for Matt, he's out of it completely, staring across the barroom like some prophet in a desert until, looking at his watch, he says to Abby, "Hey, babe, we got somewhere else to be, remember?"

Abby's jaw drops. "Oh shit, yeah. I'm sorry. We gotta go. It's been great talking to you though."

As they rise and pull themselves together, my arm slides around Angie's shoulders, pulling her toward me. A kiss on the cheek and a nuzzle of her sweet-smelling hair, and Caitlin can hardly contain herself. "Aww, I love you guys.

You're just so cute together. Hey, come and see us if you're in Morgantown again, okay? I'd just love to hear all about your road trip."

"Sure."

They wave to us in parting, except for Jeff. The last to go, he gives us one final probing look and a smile so enigmatic it ought to be painted and hung on a wall. "I hope you guys reach your promised land. It's been . . . interesting."

Wow. Well, that was just loaded with meaning. My eyes follow him across the room, all the way to the exit. If he's figured us out, maybe he'll write a paper on us and become renowned in his field on the strength of it. Outside of that, he's probably not a threat.

Besides, here's Angie with a look of complete contentment on her face. "You've enjoyed tonight, haven't you?"

She writes: *Yes. They were nice.*

The urge to kiss her again, right there and then, is irresistible. No one in the bar notices—or they're simply very good at hiding it.

"Come on, babe. Let's get back to the hotel."

Instead, we go for a stroll, shoulder to shoulder, arms around waists. The night is cool and the streets are still busy but we whisper and giggle, barely noticing anything around us. Eventually, we find our way back to our hotel, with me at least anticipating what's to come. This is how my life ought to have been. It's sure as hell how it's going to be once we're free and clear.

***

Next day around midday we arrive in Lexington, the home of Keeneland. My Angie has been all sweetness, and her driving is full of confidence. Well, mostly. It's been a good morning with no reason to suppose the rest of the day won't be the same. Added to that, the weather is growing steadily warmer so we're both wearing our summer outfits, with Angie's shawl carefully arranged to hide the joins, so to speak. As we look for somewhere to eat, we pass the Mary Todd Lincoln house.

"You wanna go visit? Could be interesting."

Angie turns her nose up at it. She'd rather go fritter our money away at the races. Gambling is the kind of risk that's never appealed to me. On the other hand, she's been so good since our little trial of wills. She deserves a reward. What the hell then. Let's go to Keeneland and blow some cash, just not too much.

We arrive just in time to miss the first race. Arm in arm, we walk from the Jeep to within sight of the entrance. Crap! They're searching purses and bags, and the .38 is right there in mine.

"Oh, hell. We gotta go back."

She looks at me like that line in front of us is for the last lifeboat on the *Titanic*.

"I forgot something, okay? Don't worry about it. We've got all afternoon. There are plenty more races."

Back at the Jeep, she's too busy fretting about missing the next race to notice as the .38 is hidden away. As soon as it's done she drags me back, through the entrance and along to the paddock, eager to see the runners. We each pick one and place our bets, just enough to make it interesting. As we watch from the grandstand, my horse leads all the way to the straight. I'm becoming quite excited . . . until Angie's horse surges past mine to win easily at the post.

"Well done! We almost both won, didn't we?"

While there's a big hug for her, the second bit is entirely for me. Never mind. We collect her winnings and pick in the third. This time it's win, place, or show for me. Angie of course goes all out to win again, and her runner goes all out to win too. Mine might just as well have stayed home, with my enthusiasm as its houseguest. As we pick up her winnings for the second time, from only a modest start, she's already made it to over a hundred dollars. This two-time loser is just trying not to sound jealous.

We pick again in the fourth, with me making a half-hearted attempt to talk her out of her selection. "But this one's got all the form, and it has such a sweet name too."

She's having none of it, determinedly staking all her winnings on her choice and, my God, she wins again.

My alarm bells are starting to twitch now, and it's got nothing to do with being a bad loser. Nor is it the freakishness of this kid from the streets who's probably never been near a horse before somehow picking three winners in a row. She's more than doubling her winnings from race to race. One more win and she'll have reached the point where the IRS will be taking an interest. That means a form to fill in and a valid photo ID to be produced. She still doesn't have one, and that has suddenly become an issue. There's always mine, of course, but it's me the Deep Web is looking for. My face is probably on some database somewhere, with facial recognition software scanning through CCTV images from all over the country to find me.

As we collect her winnings again, she's hardly able to contain herself. Security cameras and guards who might be hovering a little too close are the only things on my mind. There's nothing that seems suspicious, but still, this was foolish. This should never have been agreed to. Men's brains are supposed to turn to mush at the sight of a pretty face, not mine.

"We're leaving."

What a difference two little words can make. She wants to bet on the next race but mean mom won't let her. Mean mom is bad and never lets her do what she wants, and all that good behavior disappears like a puff of smoke. Now it's all pouting and shrugging off and, if she could talk, probably a full-on, "You're horrible and I hate you!" scene. Thankfully, it's not another trial of wills, but still she has to be hauled back to the Jeep as willingly as a dragged dog.

"I said we could go racing and we went racing. Now, stop being such a pain!"

She continues to wriggle and squirm, but it's the Jeep that's on my mind now. We've driven it for long enough. It has to go. The Blue Grass Airport is just across Route 60. That should mean rentals. A change of clothes is required, something businesslike, while the Jeep is hidden away in some quiet corner. By the time the Deep Web has wasted an hour or more looking for a mother and daughter, this frazzled executive will have disappeared into flyover country.

"Wait here, and don't talk to any strangers."

Yawning expansively, she slumps into her seat. My God, she is asking for such a slapping. If this is what being a real mom is like, from now on, my respect will be never-ending.

That's it for admiring all things mommy. Now there's a bad-tempered, big-city business type who wishes she was somewhere else as she bumps and clatters her suitcase all the way to the nearest rental outlet. A few minutes later she's standing in front of something red in the middle of the lot. It's modest, it's characterless, and it would fail miserably in a chase. At least it's got four wheels and an engine, and nobody will be looking for it until it's not returned.

Back with Angie, together, we empty the Jeep. We need to put some miles between us and Lexington before we even think of a hotel for the night. For the next few hours, we head west through farmland, forest, Louisville, and the silent treatment. Oh yes, Angie might not have a voice, but she can still do the silent treatment.

Evansville is our stopover for the night, and it's quite far enough for me. Any hope my punishment might end is quickly dashed though. Dinner is a deathly quiet affair and later, back in our hotel room, Angie curls up on her bed with her back to me. If she doesn't want to talk to me, well, fine. Two can play at that game, sweetie. Besides, it's been a long day. A good night's sleep migh be just what both of us needs.

CHAPTER EIGHT

C ome breakfast and we're on speaking terms again, which is to say Angie is no longer freezing me out. That's as far as it goes though. Told to hurry up so we can make an early start, she merely grins at me and maybe eats a little faster. At least she's not starting with the sulks again.

On the west side of Evansville is a supercenter. Parked up way across the lot from the entrance, once again Angie gets to stay with the car. She harrumphs expansively at that, arms tightly folded and slumping into a pout, but at least she does as she's told. That leaves me free to shop like a guy. Dressed plainly in black with a shoulder-length auburn wig so no one will notice me, it's a quick in and out with sneakers, sweatpants, and hoodies. There are also canvas carryalls to replace our suitcases and the baggiest coat on the rails for me. The frazzled executive they must now be looking for needs to change things up. Some gender fluidity should do it. It will be nothing for Angie to go back to being a boy. The brother he never knew he had will have to cover up and bro up though.

From there we share the driving, me first and then Angie. While she's at the wheel, my thoughts begin to wander. As tiring as yesterday was, sleep did not come easily last night. Unresolved issues crowded in, one after another, all of them demanding answers. The simplest to deal with is the ID problem. Angie needs one, and it wouldn't hurt to have a new one for me as well. For that, we need a city.

The biggest one west of us is St. Louis, so that's where we're headed. Just like everywhere else, the Network has contacts there, or it did. The Deep Web got to my contact in New York. How much further they've infiltrated is anyone's guess. It's a risk that has to be taken.

What comes next is not so easy to deal with. We've come far together in two and a half days, Angie and me, and not just in the distance we've traveled. She has become . . . what, my child, my lover? Both. It must have sounded like both to those people in Harrisburg. My God, a lesbian pedo sex orgy, right there in the room next to us, and we had to lie awake all night listening to it.

It was lust. It had to be. It still is. Admitting to something as chaotic and uncontrolled as love is simply not in me. Yet here we are, with her sitting just a hand's reach away and me feeling like drowning at the very thought she might not be. Okay, that sounds an awful lot like a besotted teenager in the grip of a high school crush, but it's still true. She might not feel the same way about me though. This might all be just some big adventure to her, something better than living on the street. At some point, once it's all been figured out and everything is just right, we will sit down and she will understand.

Or she'll laugh in my face. She would have every right to as well. My puppy, my toy, my slave; all of it borne without a word of complaint. Something is keeping her with me in spite of that, something hidden, like the deep hurt she refuses to talk about. It's there lurking in the background, passing unseen except to another girl who once suffered betrayal and loss. She knew something was wrong, some hidden truth no one wanted to talk about. Finally forcing it out, she survived it because she had to; because there was no other choice. Reflected in the glass of our hotel room window her face stares back at me, hovering like some ghost above the street lights beyond.

Ghosts, long buried but, like Angie's, still lurking there in the background. My parents, their faces only vaguely remembered after twenty years. If they were to appear before me now, they would be recognized and then they would be asked if they had been watching my progress through this life. They would be asked if they liked the daughter they gave to the world, the killer populating their little corner of Hell. There must be an awful lot of lost souls down there forever demanding an apology because of what you made me.

Forgiveness; Hell isn't big on that, and neither is your daughter. You come to me bringing nothing but anger and hurt. That makes me the victim here, and victims have the right to demand justice. Victims have the right to see their victimizers humbled and destroyed. To hell with forgiveness then. It's mine to give or withhold. You left me as you made me, with nothing but my own wits, to make the best of it. That best was to provide a service. If it hadn't been me, it would have been someone else. It was someone else who paid for it too; someone else who decided that such and such a person should die because—

Angie tugs at my sleeve. We've come to a stop in the middle of the road. There's woodland to the left and farmland to the right, the boondocks on meth. Another car is stopped maybe twenty feet ahead of us, with a woman standing by it looking like she's so relieved.

Anyone else might think she's broken down and the cell service out here is terrible. My first thought is does this rental have GPS tracking? Probably not, but that doesn't mean they haven't found us. They have eyes in the sky, after all. They could have been tracking us ever since Lexington, just waiting for somewhere nice and quiet to stage the hit.

"Stay here, okay? Do not get out of the car."

A few steps take me close enough to be within easy range. Also taking a step forward, she smiles, oh so grateful that somebody finally happened along.

"Oh, hi. Thank you so much for stopping. My car just died on me. I only had it serviced a couple of weeks back too. Our local guy doesn't usually miss things but I guess everyone has their off days, right?"

She's good, almost as good as me, but the .38 hidden in my hand has the safety off.

"Died? What do you mean, died?"

She's a short-haired blonde with an open face and an average build. She's wearing jeans with ankle boots and a thin woolen top underneath a quilted jacket. In other words, she's studiedly ordinary and my grip tightens on the .38. Most of any plan is how to get close enough before the target even knows they're in danger.

Seeing my coolness, her smile fades a little. "Well, it just sort of spluttered and died, y'know. I don't know much about cars, but it sounded like a blocked fuel line to me."

You don't know much about cars, except for perfectly describing a blocked fuel line. Seems to me somebody should have thought that story through a whole lot better. Looking her over again, the only place she could be carrying is tucked into the back of her jeans. "So exactly what kind of help were you looking for? Because we got somewhere else to be."

"Well, I'm sure I don't want to inconvenience you. I was just hoping maybe you could give me a lift to the next town. Then I can arrange for a tow truck or something."

Right! Hayseed Jane here says yes like an unsuspecting fool, and then you waltz on over and shoot us both point-blank in the face. Really, sweetie. You should have paid more attention in assassin school because the only way this was ever going to work was if you had a sniper hidden in those trees.

"I can pay you if you'd like. I have cash. I'm not asking for a free ride."

She begins to reach underneath her coat right around in back of her jeans. Before she can draw on me the .38 puts two rounds in her chest. She's barely hit the tarmac before my hands are searching for her weapon. There isn't one. There is a small wallet in one of her back pockets containing a driver's license and about fifty bucks. Crap! She's a civilian, and now there's a storm brewing, complete with the threat of thunder and lightning, and its name is Angie. She's standing beside me looking down on precisely what she was never meant to see. That storm could become a full-on hurricane, and there's no one to blame for it but me, the professional killer who let paranoia get the better of her.

That's all the guilt there's time for. Now the fallout has to be dealt with. The road both ways is still empty. For so long as it stays that way, there's a way out of this. The problem is Angie. Wide-eyed and open-mouthed, she's horrified. That's understandable. It's not every day a person gets to watch Mommy gun down a total stranger in cold blood. She has to get over it though, and quickly.

"Listen to me, baby. Listen to me."

She doesn't. There's nothing for it but to take a firm hold and shake her, just enough to make her look at me. "Angie, listen to me. This was a mistake; that's all, just a terrible mistake. I got it wrong, okay? But what's done is done. We can stand here feeling sorry about it or we can clean it up before somebody comes by and sees it. Do you hear me?"

She hears me, but her horror turns first to disbelief and then disgust. She tries to shake my hands off, but that's not happening. "No! You listen to me. This isn't about being sent back into the system anymore. If somebody comes along right now, it's a life sentence for murder, with you as an accessory, or I shoot them too. Look, I'm sorry, really I am, but right now, you have to choose. Either you help me or you go down with me. We can still get out of this, baby. We can still have everything I promised you, but you have to choose and you have to choose now."

She stops trying to fight me. Now she's glaring at me, cold and hard, because once more she's been betrayed. Well, maybe she has, but that isn't going to get us out of this. "You have to choose, Angie. We can still have it all but only if you help me."

Slowly, her glare lessens. She glances at the body. She looks at me. We are not in a good place, but dealing with that will have to wait. Getting us out of here is the only thing that matters right now, and as fast as possible. "Help me. We have to get her into the car and the car into the trees. By the time anyone finds her, we'll be a long way from here. Now come on, help me lift her."

She's a lot calmer, but still reluctant.

"Angie. Come on!"

Just as it seems she might have to be slapped out of it, at last, she responds. Together, we lift the body. More by trial and error than anything else, we sit it in the driver's seat, then slowly push the car off the road and deep into the trees. The only evidence left for any passerby to see is a bloodstain on the pavement. Most will probably not even notice, and those that do will probably call it roadkill. In a way, it was.

★★★

We reach the outskirts of St. Louis just after midday. The journey has passed in a foreboding silence. Both of us had ghosts already. Now we have one to share. It's almost sitting there between us, like the Berlin Wall.

The parking lot of a supercenter will lose the rental for a while. It will also allow us to change into hoodies and sweatpants as far as possible from any watching eyes. With my baggy coat done up to the collar, we do pass for brothers; very young brothers. How easy it's been to forget just how young my beautiful Angie really is. Now, for a while at least, she's gone. The feeling of loss is already affecting me, which is rather silly, since she's standing right there in front of me. All we have to do when it's safe again is take her out of the closet, so to speak. Until then, there's a certain sweetness to it, like dreaming of ice cream on a desert island.

Carryalls over our shoulders, we cross Carlyle Avenue into the college. From here we can catch the MetroLink into the center of St. Louis. A little over half an hour later, we are outside the convention center. Now we need a hotel. For that, one of us has to be an adult. There's a parking structure in Convention Plaza. In a quiet corner, one of the boys who caught the MetroLink becomes a mom again. In our red dress, a blonde wig, and make up; this mom now has a son. If anyone asks, his name is Angelo.

There's a hotel nearby. It's reasonable, but that's the least of my concerns. As he walks before me along the corridor, his shoulders are hunched beneath a weight of woe. One misjudged act was all it took, one knee-jerk reaction by the killer within. This is not the time for regret though, and even less so for guilt. They are bloodstains on the pavement, mere history, like all my other kills. If only that were true. Not so long ago, it would have been. Guilt and regret wouldn't have even got a foot through the door. Now his desolation has thrown that door open and grinning at me behind those two unwelcome guests is the thought of losing him forever.

Inside our room, the carryalls are dumped on the floor. He sits on the edge of the bed, eyes downcast, more lost than he's ever been. Watching him only makes it worse. Every moment of it allows that deep hurt within him to begin to tear at me. Guilt and regret lurk in the corner, but this cannot be about them. This is about staying in control. This is about keeping us one step ahead of the Deep Web and not losing him along the way.

Beside him on the bed, my hand reaches for one of his. "Baby, I'm so sorry. I thought she had a weapon. I just didn't want to take the chance."

He continues to sit, head bowed and unresponsive. He might not even be listening. "I promised you I wouldn't let anyone hurt you ever again. Well, maybe I was too quick to judge. Maybe I just panicked a little. We all make mistakes, sweetheart, just usually not such final ones. I'm sorry; I'm not trying to make light of it. It was horrible, and I get how you feel. Really, I do."

If only he would open up to me. There might never be a better moment than now, while he's so vulnerable. "Look, I know you've seen me do some things: in New York and Harrisburg and on our way here. I didn't do any of those things because I like violence, you know. I really am only trying to protect us."

Nothing. He might just as well be deaf as well as dumb. "Baby, I know what it feels like when your world is turned upside down, and I know you do too. My parents, well, they did things they shouldn't have and no one stopped them. No one protected me. Maybe no one protected you either. Maybe that's how you got hurt. I know someone hurt you. I saw it in your eyes that day I took you home."

Still nothing, and, over there in the corner, guilt and regret have become a pair of puffer fish, google-eyed and growing fat as they suck up my self-confidence. "Yes, I know I hurt you too, but I was angry. That guy on the High Line, well, you saw how he stabbed me. I know you watched the news. I shot him too, but I was defending myself. You do understand that, don't you? Then the police came, and I lied to them, and it all just grew and grew. I didn't know what to do except that we had to get away. I was scared, Angie. We're all scared when people hurt us, especially when it's those people we ought to be able to trust the most. Those are the wounds that never heal. We just bury them and then they end up controlling us, you and me both."

Please, Angie, at least look at me. At least see how this is hurting me too. Your pain is my pain; your loss is my loss. Share it with me, because you are not alone. Trust me and you will never be alone again. My hand slides across the back of his shoulders. They are taut, frozen, as impossible to soothe as his silence. "Sweetheart, please talk to me. I've told you why I did what I did, and I'm sorry I involved you in it. But that's not what matters here. All of that, we can figure out later. Baby, I just want you to be happy. I want us to be happy. So tell me. Tell me something, no matter how little it is. We can work it out together and then put it behind us forever. We can—"

Suddenly, he leaps to his feet and stalks across the room, pacing back and forth like a bored tiger hating on all the faces beyond the glass. It's an act of violence in itself, a rejection that leaves me stunned.

"Angie?"

He points a finger at me, bluntly accusatory, and mouths the words: *"You kill people!"*

"Angie, I already told you—"

"No!"

He takes a step toward me, fixes me with a glare and demands: *"How many?"*

That's a truth that dare not be told, not while he's like this, anyway. If only that woman had broken down somewhere else. If only the killer within me hadn't seized control, and right there in front of him too. Empty wishes don't matter though. His demand has to be answered and, just as in Allentown, that answer has to be the least that can be gotten away with.

"Two. I've killed two. Honestly, Angie, I've only ever tried to—"

He doesn't believe me. If he could make a sound, he might be crowing his disbelief. Instead, he takes out his notepad and begins to write. Screwing up the words as if they are beyond offensive to him, he throws them across the room at me. It's pure disgust, perhaps even contempt, and the note itself says: *dumb ain't stupid.*

More notes quickly follow: *I think you like it. I think you get off on it. I think you're lying to me.*

"Angie, I've never done anything I didn't have to do to survive."

He comes at me again, this time two paces, and demands: *how many!*

His anger is beginning to infect me, or maybe it's my own rage reawakening.

"Okay! I killed my parents. There, are you happy now? I killed them because they made me what I am. I was a child. I was alone and hurting. I had no one to turn to. I didn't know what else to do. I did it because I wanted them to know what it felt like. They died instead. You think I wanted that? I didn't want that. I wanted them to say sorry. I wanted them to admit to what they did. Instead, they left me to live with it, and I did because what else was I supposed to do?"

What? What did your parents do to you?

"What did your parents do to you?"

His glare turns bitterly cold. He makes as if to write another note, but he's beyond disgusted now. Those last words were a mistake, a terrible mistake. Whatever happened to him, it wasn't his parents who were to blame, but it's almost too late to put it right. He's heading for the door. He's leaving. No. You will not walk out on me. "Angie!"

The door is open. He's walking through it.

"Angie, stop!"

Panic grips me, the kind of unthinking headlong panic that has me chasing after him, grabbing his arm and forcing him to stop and face me. "Angie, please. I'm sorry, all right? I'm sorry I said that. Please, baby, just come back. We can work this out. We can take our time. We can help each other, but not if you walk away. Think about it, Angie. Where are you going to go? Who's going to look after you?"

Slowly, his anger begins to subside. There is no more hate-filled glare, but he isn't won back yet. He is waiting, cold and judgmental. He wants something more, something beyond a mere apology. My panic falls away too because suddenly, everything is clear. His forgiveness is all that matters to me. Ask anything, demand anything, just please don't walk out on me. "Please, Angie, come back. Don't you understand? I love you. We   "

For an instant, time freezes. Twenty-four hours ago those words seemed ridiculous. Now it feels like they've always been true, and this fool was just too stupid to realize it. He moved into my head, and then into my apartment, and the influence he held over me that mystified me was love at first sight. Even now it sounds ridiculous, but here we are with me now waiting for him to answer and hoping he will not just laugh at me and keep walking. Instead, he mouths the words: *"No more killing. No more."*

"No more. I swear." So long as it can be avoided. If it can't, well, we'll have to deal with that when it happens. For now, he pulls me into an embrace, and his forgiveness is mine. This is a threshold we have crossed. What lies beyond is still fraught with danger, but it seems to me we both know there is now an unspoken agreement between us. Neither of us will talk of these things again until we're ready, until we're past the hurt and the anger.

As we stand in the middle of the corridor locked in our embrace, some guy walks past. With half a glance and half a smile, he says, "Jeez, guys, get a room."

CHAPTER NINE

We rise sometime around midmorning. Neither of us cares, even though there are things to do. The previous night has passed in tenderness and affirmation, and watching him dress now makes me feel secure, despite the silliness of it. He's not my protector. He's barely even a man, and he's certainly not muscular. No one would call him a fighter, although he has filled out since New York. He is lean with youth, almost athletic in his litheness, and that just makes me love him even more.

In return, he smiles as he looks at me, open and uncomplicated. There is my security, the knowing that he will not leave. He ought to, because it's not him the Deep Web is hunting. If he chose to, he wouldn't want for anything, either. He would have the world at his feet. That would be my gift to him: a fortune salted away in havens across the world. But he will not do that. This is our journey now; however it may end, be it captured or clear across the border into Mexico.

Once we're both dressed, me in turtleneck, pants, and my auburn wig, he in hoodie and sneakers, we go out. We're just a mom and her darling boy saying hi to the Gateway City. We should have a couple of days in St. Louis before we need to be concerned. Even if the Deep Web has tracked us to the rental place at Blue Grass Airport, it's going to have to find that car and the body inside. By the time they find the rental out by the college, St. Louis will be a memory for us.

Not that we'll be wasting any time. The sooner we're out of here, the better. That means arrangements to be made: fake IDs to be found and bus tickets to be bought. That means we're going shopping. What better way to spend what's left of the day, or so it seems to me. Angie probably sees it differently, but then he can't exactly start mouthing off about it.

We take one carryall with us. It contains most of our money, wrapped up in my boy clothes just in case anyone tries to peek. The .38 is in my purse. Yes, my promise to Angie still stands, and, yes, it should have been dumped by now since it's no longer clean. Until we can buy another gun, though, it's the only protection we have.

The other carryall stays in our room. It contains all of Angie's bits and pieces and most of our girl clothes. We'll collect that later, after all the arrangements have been made.

First of all, we need a burner phone. An internet café is next so our bus tickets can be booked. We'll be heading for Oklahoma City. We could go farther. We could go all the way to El Paso, but a day and a half on a bus is too much of a risk. Eleven hours is risk enough. So, just to be sure, the Deep Web will be dummied into thinking we've gone somewhere else. Portland should be distracting enough. Those tickets will be bought at the bus station before we board.

By now, it's midday, and we find somewhere to eat. Sat by a window, while Angie watches the world go by, my call to the local contact goes in. The number's dead. Either the Deep Web has taken down the entire Network, or everyone's gone dark. Never mind. Contacts never meet, unless they're also suppliers. Then, it can't be avoided, especially when it's IDs that are being supplied. We'll head on over after lunch. That gives me another opportunity to try to get some more information out of Angie; some of it a necessity. Just don't go near that thing we're not talking about.

"So, what do you think of St. Louis?"

Nice; could stay here.

"Really? Better than the Big Apple?"

He shrugs. *A street's a street.*

Nice try, kid, but you don't kill the conversation that easily, not when you're talking to me. "But you're not on the street. You're with me, and we're going to have a good life together."

He doesn't seem all that convinced.

"I've gotten us this far, haven't I? Okay, I've made some mistakes along the way. I'm sorry for that. But, once we're across the border, we can go anywhere we want. First of all, though, we have to get you some documents. To do that, you're going to have to give me some details, like your date of birth."

He shrugs again. *Why? Fake is fake.*

"Why? We can't very well turn up at immigration claiming you're twenty-five if you're only fifteen. It's fake, not pure fantasy. I'm gonna need the state you were born in too."

He thinks about that for a moment. *Hawaii.*

"Hawaii. Really? You expect me to believe you, a mute kid from Hawaii, somehow made it to New York all on your own. Are you going to tell me you swam halfway across the Pacific as well?"

He decides to brazen it out. *Might have.*

My daughter was so much more amenable, except when she was acting up, of course. At least when she invented answers they were reasonable, like coming from upstate New York. "Well, fine then. If you're just gonna sit there and stonewall me, you're eighteen and you're from New York. Don't come complaining to me about it later."

He flourishes the okay sign at me, like, it's all cool, baby. The hint of smugness in it doesn't impress me, but never mind. Lunch is as good as over and there are more important things that need dealing with.

***

We leave the diner and stroll through downtown, picking up our bus tickets along the way. The place we're heading for is off Washington, a computer repair shop, or at least that's what the sign outside says. The real business is in back, hiding in plain sight amongst all the motherboards and hard drives and such; just a nerd nirvana to the unsuspecting eye.

The owner watches us enter. His eye is anything but unsuspecting. It's the kind of eye that can spot the difference between an undercover cop and a customer at fifty feet. As we approach, the look he's giving me is something else, like the unclean just arrived, bells ringing and all.

"Hey."

"Hey." His eye moves to Angie because, y'know, the unclean always travel in pairs.

"Yeah, I got a problem with my laptop, something to do with the ID, I think. If I was to bring it in—"

He cuts in, surly as a cornered cat, "Sorry, lady. Can't help you."

"You can't help me? But—"

"Listen. The best I can do for you is be deaf, dumb, and blind. I got a legit business to run here, and I got the right to refuse service, so why don't you scram before you bring the wrong kind of attention down on me. Understand?"

As clear as day, sweetie, as clear as day. The Network has not just gone dark; it's turned its back on me. As far as it's concerned, this ex-coworker is persona non grata, an untouchable, an actual leper.

We leave, walking back along Washington toward the Mississippi. Angie is writing notes. They all say much the same. *What now?* Patience, kid. Stuff like this doesn't get dealt with in five minutes, especially when one eye is trying to keep tabs on whether the repair shop was staked out or not. There's no obvious sign of it, but then they probably don't need to. It's a fair bet computer repair guy is calling someone, and that means St. Louis is no longer safe. Hanging around waiting for a bus is no longer an option. We need a new plan and a quicker exit. As for those IDs, for now, they're on the back burner—

"What?" That's for Angie, who's started tugging at my sleeve.

He points across the street. There's a group of women on the sidewalk. They're handing out leaflets, noisily, especially when a man chooses to ignore them. They're also multicolored, a regular rainbow alliance, each one with hair of a different color: red, blue, green, orange, and purple. It's not hard to figure they're some kind of feminist collective, and that gives me an idea. My Network may have disowned me, but the sisterhood is there for all of us, right? This poor, helpless woman is a victim of the big, bad patriarchy, otherwise known as the Deep Web. My daughter is too—or she will be once she's dressed up nice and looking innocent again. This could be just the gift we need, and if it leads to nothing, well, something else will surely come along.

We cross over. One of them thrusts a leaflet at me. That's okay. This sister is all for solidarity—so long as it serves my interests, of course. What the leaflet is about is neither here nor there. The contact number is all that matters, and a good story to tell when it's used.

From there, we stroll around downtown some more, pausing to browse store windows and occasionally going in. Come mid-afternoon, we go for coffee and my story is all figured out. Now to work the sisterhood, starting with my best poor little hurt and lost voice when the phone is answered. "Hello? Hello, can you help us?"

"Can we help you with what?" This sister is decidedly less than sympathetic. "Who are you?"

"I can't tell you over the phone. They might be listening. But I'm here with my daughter and we desperately need help. Can you help us?"

"They?" She's becoming pricklier. "Who are they?"

"My husband. He has powerful friends. You know who they are; the privileged, the old white men, the abusers."

"If you need a shelter, I can—"

"No, please. We can't go to a shelter. The authorities know where the shelters are. They'll find us like they did before. Please, I'm begging you. Let me talk to you in person. I'll tell you everything and then, if you still don't want to help us, we'll leave."

The line goes quiet. This sister must have an über sister to report to. Hoping that list of trigger words hasn't overplayed my hand, for the next minute or so my newfound feminist outrage is downloaded, installed, and set to default, until at last the voice returns. "Okay. Do you have a pen and paper? Here's our address. Come by around seven."

"Thank you. Thank you so much. You don't know how much this means to us. We'll be there at seven."

So far, so good. We have a few hours to kill, which gives us plenty of time to prepare. As we stroll back to our hotel, what to do about Angie has to be decided. He could become she again, or another layer of victimhood could be slapped on. He's already mute. He could be early-stage transitioning as well. Without knowing how radical this collective is, it's all just a toss of a coin.

All such thoughts fly as we round a corner into Convention Plaza and join the back of the small crowd that's gathered outside our hotel. There are three cruisers in front, all half parked up on the sidewalk with their lights flashing. What the hell? This could be a coincidence, or my bet was good. Computer repair guy did call someone. Deaf, dumb, and blind, huh. Weasel! Needing to know either way, we join the back of the crowd, quite a lot of them with their phones out videoing it all.

"Hey, man, you know what's goin' down?"

"Probably a stiff. People die in hotels all the time."

"Awful lotta cops for a stiff, ain't it? And what's the hurry?"

"Maybe it's a fugitive then, like someone they've been after for a while."

"Whatever it is, I hope something's gonna happen soon. I wanna get this uploaded before anyone else."

Right then, a black SUV glides to the curb. Four suits get out. They just have to be Deep Web. Computer repair guy did rat us out. That can only mean one thing. The Deep Web and the Network are working together. It could be an alliance or a straight-out take over, but it hardly matters. What does matter is the sheer speed with which they got from weasel to our hotel. Like, wow! Just think of the resources they must be throwing into finding me. If only the poor shmucks knew. Perhaps a big wave and a, "Hey guys, over here!" would help. Then again, perhaps not.

At the same time, Angie tugs at my sleeve again, nodding that we should walk away. He's right, of course. This is no place for probably the most wanted woman in the country to be. As for that carryall we left in the room, we have no choice but to kiss it goodbye. There's nothing in it that cannot be replaced, and maybe all those cops and suits will have a laugh or two figuring out what was going on in that room.

In the parking structure that's become my walk-in closet, Angie's brother makes his return. For the next couple of hours, we loiter. Sitting in doorways or hanging on street corners, we pass ourselves off as vagrants. Sometimes Angie holds out his hand, just to make it look good. Most people ignore us, some are positively irritated, but every once in a while someone drops us some change or maybe even a few dollars. Occasionally, someone will stop and talk to us, ask us how we got here and tell us where the shelters are. My best boy voice feeds them a tale. "Nah, we're just passing through. Waitin' for our ride, y'know? Don't worry about it. We're good."

As seven approaches, we catch a cab and head on out to the suburbs. The address is a two-story house, red brick with a dormer window on top. It stands at the top of a short slope with steps leading up to a porch. The grass and shrubs on either side are uncut and the paintwork on the white door and window frames is cracked and peeling. It's all in need of a little care and attention, but never mind. It's the hearts that lie within that matter; all those feelings just waiting to be exploited.

Before we begin, Angie must be made presentable. Circumstances have forced my hand. He's early-stage transitioning. With his hair frizzed out, a little mascara and eyeliner would be good but we lost those in the raid. Besides, this is supposed to be a desperate escape from all that white male privilege, not a gay pride parade.

At the top of the steps, a young woman opens the door. She's sturdily built, with red hair, tats, and a ring through her nose. She looks us over, Angie in particular. "I thought you said you had your daughter with you."

"She is my daughter. She's only just started transitioning."

She looks at Angie again. She sniffs. Awkward. Of course, it was always possible we might end up amongst a nest of TERFs, but then the coin hasn't landed yet. When at last it does, instead of slamming the door in our faces, she waves us in. Off a passage leading to the back is the living room. It too could do with some attention: its paintwork stale and cracked, its plaster flaking, its furniture and rugs worn threadbare. Seated on two couches before us is the entire rainbow collective. Their heads are all turned. Their eyes are without emotion. They are watching us like a jury. The judge sits opposite, in the only single chair in the room. It's a very big chair, dwarfing the elderly lady who occupies it. Probably in her sixties, with short, gray hair, she is still quietly commanding: the matriarch who must be respected. That's fine by me. She, and the rest of them, can have as much respect as they want. Hell, they can have groveling and fawning if that's what it takes to win their trust.

"Thank you. Thank you for letting us come."

The matriarch gestures, and room is made for us on a couch. The jury continues to watch, like birds of prey waiting for the falconer to unleash them.

For a minute or so this falconer takes us in, her gaze as searching as a dentist's probe. "So you want us to help you, do you? You say you can't tell us anything over the phone because *they* might be listening. You can't go to a shelter because they will find you and you bring a boy here you say is transitioning. Perhaps you ought to tell us why we shouldn't just throw you back out onto the street."

Purposefully, my words struggle to come out. "Yes . . . I'm sorry . . . Really, I wouldn't have come to you but . . . we're in trouble, serious trouble. When I saw you on the sidewalk this afternoon . . . I didn't know where else to turn. I—"

"Yes, yes, yes. I think we're all waiting for the meat and potatoes. I'm sorry. That just came out. We're all vegans here, so I apologize if I've offended anyone. Now, why do you want our help, and who is it you're so afraid of?"

My hands wring with reluctance. My voice begins to tremble. "You remember that guy who died suddenly a few days ago in Washington, the one they said could've been president?"

"Indeed. It was an embolism, wasn't it?"

"No. It wasn't." A perfectly timed pause lets the tension build. "I . . . I was his wife. I shot him. I killed him. The government covered it all up. We are the only ones left who know the truth, and they want to silence us."

The hush is deathly, with half the collective leaning forward to hang upon my every word while the other half exchange knowing glances. Typical! The patriarchy at its worst. You can't trust any of them. The matriarch remains a harder nut to crack. That's why she's the one sitting in the big chair.

"Really. How convenient of the government to cover it all up. But then, I suppose they can say anything they like, can't they? As can you. I seem to recall the family asked to be left in peace. Remind me, would you: how many children were there?"

Bitch! Of all the questions she could've asked, this is the one that hadn't occurred to me. Okay. Not a problem. Just cover it up. Take Angie by the hand and look distraught while my brain frantically searches for the answer. Come on. The lawyer said this, right there on screen. He leaves a wife, a wife and . . . and . . . two children. There were two children. "I . . . I had to leave my daughter behind. She was innocent in all of this. God, I don't know if I'll ever see her again!"

The collective is beginning to wilt like day-old lettuce, but not the matriarch.

"Well, that's all very unfortunate. But while I can sympathize with any woman who sees fit to shoot her husband, I still don't see why we should help you. Perhaps you ought to go to a shelter. I'm sure they'll be able to find you a good lawyer."

"No, you don't understand. My husband was right-wing, very right-wing. He was a conservative and a traditionalist. He—"

"He wanted to abolish abortion?" says one of the girls.

"No!" says another, horrified. "Not Roe v. Wade. Cocksucker!"

Almost letting slip with "Yes, he was one of those too," instead, my dead "husband" becomes the very devil himself. "It's worse than that. This is my daughter . . . well, now my other daughter, Angie. She told me some time ago that she was transgender. I've been helping her for a while in secret but my husband, whatever else he might have been, wasn't stupid. He figured it out. He realized his son was going to become his daughter. He just couldn't handle that. It went against everything he stood for: his politics, his religion, his family name. He went ballistic. I thought he was going to kill both of us. I had no choice. I was defending myself. I was defending my daughter. And now his powerful friends are covering it up. They don't want that kind of thing getting out. Better for them if he just died suddenly, the man who could have been president. Except for us. We're the only ones left who know, and they want to silence us."

Oh my God, the violence, the privilege, the sheer old white maleness of it! There's hardly a girl sitting around me without a hand to her mouth or eyes wide with horror. They're mine. Only the matriarch remains to be won over. She's a tough old bird; that can't be denied. But there's still one more card up my sleeve. Angie. Sitting there beside me, with his eyes firmly stuck on the floor and thinking who knows what, he looks so vulnerable and lost that any heart must surely melt at the sight of it. Just to make sure they do, slathering on comfort and reassurance like it's mayo on everything, my hand squeezes his while the other rises to brush his cheek. "Don't worry, baby. Everything will be fine."

"Oh, please," bursts a green-haired girl. "Please can we help them?"

"Yes," chimes in another, with orange hair. "I mean, they're Nazis, and transphobic, and they probably want to put all those poor, little undocumented children into concentration camps. We must help them to expose the patriarchy for what it really is. We simply must, mustn't we?"

The matriarch hears their pleas but continues to watch me. She's wearing a wry little smile, suggesting she knows she's being played. It doesn't matter because now she has to take into account the mood of the collective as well, and where they stand is clear. The choice is simple. She can either slap down her foolish followers, or she can allow them this little indulgence and wait for another day, another cause, with which to impose her will.

"Very well. Since my girls are so taken with you, and I suppose they do have a point. How can you expose these terrorists if they've made you disappear? How exactly can we help you, then? What is it that you need?"

"Oh, thank you. We need a way out of St. Louis. I won't tell you where we're headed, but anywhere west or south. We've been lucky so far, but I don't know how close behind us they are. New IDs would help as well: passports and such. I have money. I can pay for them."

"I can help you with that." This girl has cropped purple hair and muscles alongside all the ironwork and tats. As tough as she may look though, she doesn't move a finger until the matriarch has given her the nod. "I'll make a couple of calls; see what I can rustle up."

"Well. I guess you'll be staying the night then. You and your daughter will have to share a room, I'm afraid, but you'll be safe. We don't allow men in, except under exceptional circumstances."

The matriarch's smile has become inscrutable. She knows what she knows, and the rest of us can only guess. My guess is, she's wondering if my hands will wander during the night. She might even be hoping for it so that her gullible flock can see the fraud unmasked. Well, not tonight. Tonight, Mommy's going to be a good girl.

CHAPTER TEN

The next day sees the collective fall even further under my spell. They are more than willing listeners, lapping up my stories of oppression and victimhood like the milk they'll one day be feeding their cats.

The same cannot be said of the matriarch. From a certain distance, she watches over her brood with a vague smile and guiding comments if asked. My words are listened to without challenge, but it's no more than toleration. She knows a budding rival when she sees one, and she won't be at all sorry to see the back of us.

As for Angie, most of them seem quite taken with him, especially once they find out he's mute. His place on the victim hierarchy just went stratospheric, but that's fine by me. Just another one of the girls, he plays along willingly enough. It isn't that hard. He's been playing the girl for most of our journey from New York.

Come mid-morning and there's a sharp knock at the front door. Crop-haired purple girl—or Gabs, as she calls herself—answers it, and the rest of them disappear to their rooms. It's a man: tough-looking, raspy-leather-jacket-wearing, flinty-eyed with a thick mustache and slicked-down hair. The disappeared must view him as an invasion of their safe space. Gabs is less fragile. She's as familiar with him as a partner in crime and introduces him to us as Ray, her go-to guy. We stand on opposite sides of the living room, amidst the threadbare couches and peeling decor, eyeing each other up until he says, "So. Whaddaya need?"

"ID. Y'know, driver's licenses and passports, that kind of thing. Make my son eighteen years old and we're both from New York."

"Son?" Gabs is mildly surprised—or is it mildly offended. "I thought she was your daughter."

"Oh, she is. I just thought . . ." We lost all our girl clothes in the hotel, but she doesn't need to know that. "Well, I don't know who they're looking for exactly, y'know, a son or a daughter. I just thought it would be easier if she's my son until we're out of the country. That's all."

She seems happy enough with that. Ray doesn't care. To him, this is just business. "Anything else you need?"

"Yes. Could you get me a gun, for protection? I mean, I hope I'll never have to use it, but just in case."

Ray nods. He can do that. He quotes a price. It's a big chunk out of our funds, but quality work is worth paying for, so long as it is quality work. With half paid upfront, he sets up, takes photographs, and we're all but done.

"You want these ASAP, right?" he says to Gabs. She nods. "I'll be back this evening then."

As the front door closes behind him, one by one, the mice emerge from their nests. The next thing to be arranged is a way out of St. Louis. Once again, it's Gabs who has the connections. She makes some more phone calls. A little later, she announces that we have a ride. It's leaving at midnight for Denver. That's too far west for us so we'll be dropped off in Kansas City.

For the rest of the day, we hang with the collective. After lunch, everyone goes out into the yard. It's as unkempt as the front. We sit around in the long grass and chitchat about this and that. Somehow, it always returns to microaggressions and why everything is rape. Meanwhile, the grass grows and the paint peels. One day the house will fall down and we'll all be equal in our homelessness.

After dinner, there's a discussion group. We all sit in the living room while everybody brainstorms how they're going to overthrow the patriarchy. My answer whenever they refer to me has become a shy smile. They think that's probably due to the trauma of everything we've been through. It's not. It's because this has all become rather wearing. Besides, this sister has probably taken out more members of the patriarchy than they've had tofu burgers.

After about two hours of this, Ray returns. The Lord works in mysterious ways and his reappearance almost has me believing. For the rest of them, he's still a demon incarnate and they all scurry back to their rooms.

With Gabs and Angie either side of me, he hands over our new IDs and a 9mm. The IDs are quality work; only an

expert should be able to tell they're fake. The 9mm is clean—
his mother's life on it. If there's a sweet old lady out there
somewhere who suddenly drops dead because he's lying,
well, that's his bad, not mine. Once he's been paid what we
owe, we are left with a little over a thousand dollars.

As soon as he's gone, Gabs starts moving things
along. "Get your shit together, ladies. We'll be leaving in
half an hour."

In fact, we leave in an hour, with earnest goodbyes
and good lucks and the gift of a pussy hat for each of us to
remember them by. It's all so sweet and from the heart that
my thanks are almost convincingly heartfelt too.

Our transport is a battered, old van, in the back of
which we find room for ourselves amidst a clutter of boxes
full of leaflets, rolled-up banners, and protest boards. Gabs
drives. Riding shotgun is Aleesha, the red-haired girl we
met first. Listening to their chatter helps to pass the time. It
also makes me think it's a good thing we're all sisters here
because God help any man who tries to jump them in an
alley after dark, or anywhere else for that matter. If they
weren't members of the collective, they would probably be
very good at running their own street gang, or even a new
Network. Imagine that, a Network run by the sisterhood
for the sisterhood. There'd be no more of these screw-ups.

An hour later, we arrive at a truck stop in Foristell. We
go for coffee and discover our ride is already here. She's the
only woman in a diner full of men, apart from the staff. Our
escorts stalk toward her, almost daring all the misogynists

to kick off. It seems they have better things to do, like fuel up and hit the road. So does our ride. She stands to greet us: brunette, hair tied back, surprisingly svelte and feminine for a trucker. That'll be my internalized misogynist talking.

After we've all been introduced, she says, "Yeah, I've made good time. That's the great thing about working nights. There are no bunny hoppers to get in the way. So I'm dropping these two off in Bright Lights, right?"

"Right," says Gabs. "We'll owe you one, for the sisterhood."

"Yo, the sisterhood," says our ride. "Now drink your mud, ladies. I wanna be in Colorado before the seat covers come out."

What she's saying goes right over my head, but if she can talk the talk, that's good enough for me. One cup of coffee later and we're clean shooting I-70 to Kansas, whatever that means.

***

It's 3:00 a.m. and our ride drops us off at the junction of Independence and Walnut. It's been a mostly quiet journey, just intermittent chitchat. We've mashed the motor, kept the shiny side up, and avoided being eaten by bears, all of which are apparently good. After exchanging goodbyes, we watch as her rig heads on into the west. With the disappearance of her taillights, we are entirely alone except for the sound of other rigs passing on the highway. Beneath glaring street lights we walk up Walnut, a wide avenue lined with trees and darkened frontages, looking for somewhere to hang until dawn.

All is now silent. Some nighttime strolls are made for that. Some aren't. This one fills with the sound of me burbling on about nothing in particular. Angie plays along at being attentive, nodding and smiling whenever he thinks it's appropriate. He's not really listening, but then, it doesn't really matter. This feels like the kind of date regular people might go on. The evening is over and neither of us wants to go home so we're just dreaming of rose gardens and picket fences and how many children we'll have, so long as the world doesn't burst into flames first.

Ahead of us is a junction. On the other side is a small, decorative arch. It tells us we are about to enter the historic City Market. As we cross the street, neither of us notices the van that slides up behind us until hands grab at me and haul me inside. There isn't time to struggle or even cry out as the door slides shut on Angie. With its wheels squealing, the van roars away, and from somewhere someone screams, "No!"

It could be me because this is not happening. Whoever these scumbags are, they just picked themselves the wrong fight. There are two of them holding me down. There's at least one other driving the van, and while the first two try to control my squirming and kicking, he, or maybe a fourth, says, "Jeez, guys, come on. I thought this was your thing. Shut her down, for chrissakes."

That voice sounds very familiar. Trying to place it is enough to stop me struggling, which pleases him. "There you go. I knew you guys could do it."

The van drives on for some minutes, taking several turns as it leaves Angie far behind. Fortunately, he had our one remaining carryall, with all our money in it. Unfortunately, both the .38 and the 9mm are in it as well. Okay. This might be me alone and unarmed, but this is still one girl who isn't going to end up in some harem or drugged up in a brothel.

The van slows to a halt. Someone gets out. A gate opens. The van moves forward. A sectional door opens. The van drives through. The change in ambiance, the echo of the motor until it dies, tells me we're inside a large, enclosed space, most likely a warehouse. The side door is pulled back, and waiting for me beyond it is the owner of that familiar voice. It's Joey with the laughing eyes. "Hey, sweet cheeks. Bet you never thought you'd see me again, huh?"

You can say that again. You are one determined son of a bitch to be following me halfway across the country. That sheik, or whoever, must have offered a shitload of money to get his hands on me. Or maybe this is something else. You and me, we'll have to have a sit-down later and thrash it all out, woman to eunuch. For now, a silent glare is all he's getting out of me. Not that he and his super-white smile cares.

"Come on, guys. Let's get her strapped in. We got a lot to get through in what's left of tonight."

He leads the way, with two more of them manhandling me behind while the fourth, the driver, brings up the rear. The side wall ahead of us is stacked with pallets, all loaded up with shrink-wrapped boxes. Hidden behind one of those stacks is a trapdoor. Beneath are stairs leading down to a small basement and, look at that, they've got themselves their very own private little torture chamber. There's even a contraption in the middle of the floor to which, for all my attempts to fight them, they strip me and bind me naked. You guys must be as dumb as a box of hammers. Damaged goods ain't worth as much. Or maybe this really is something else.

As a final indignity, they ball-gag me, even though not one word has passed my lips. And then one of the two creeps who manhandled me has the nerve to say, "She don't talk much, does she."

The other one leans in to give me a closer look. "Maybe she's like one of them dolls. Y'know, they don't say anything until you stick something in the right hole. Then they don't quit."

Before their discussion can become any more philosophical, Joey decides to move things along. "Well, I guess we'll find out later. Come on, guys. There's a bottle upstairs. You go on up and crack it open. I'll be with you in a minute or two."

As they leave, Joey steps forward to lean in eyeball to eyeball. "So here's the thing. You've pissed an awful lot of people off. But never mind. Tonight we're gonna close your account, so to speak. Then all of us can get back to business as usual. It's a shame, really. I think we would've worked well together. And in case you're getting the wrong impression, this ain't my thing. This is what those chumps upstairs are into. They're useful to us so we let them have their fun. Speaking of which, I owe you an apology. I just plain forgot to bring my laser with me. I guess some big, fat boners will have to do instead. I'll be thinking of you though, and all those wonderful times we could have had together. It just breaks my heart, really it does."

He rises, patting me on the cheek like we're best pals or something. Halfway across the floor he stops, turns, and adds, "Oh, and in case you're thinking some realtor might show up and maybe try to sell this place, don't. We own it. It's one of our distribution centers, all above board and very, very ordinary as far as the wage slaves know. No one's coming to rescue you. I just thought you ought to know that. After all, it wouldn't be fair to let you get your hopes up, would it? Nope. There are no white knights riding to the rescue around here."

With that, he's gone, leaving a mystery behind him. None of what he just said sounds like trafficking. It sounds an awful lot like he's Network. We really are going to have to have a sit-down and talk this all through later.

For now though, the distant sound of them drifts down the stairs to me. They're taunting me, hoping thoughts of the very worst of what they intend to do will break me. Dream on, guys. There's a whole world of hurt waiting for you once this contraption is beaten, if it can be beaten.

Ignoring their far-off laughter, all my effort goes into breaking free. There must be a way. If only my bonds weren't so tight. If only their fixings weren't so firm. If only—

Frustration begins to give way to hopelessness. Joey chose his words well and, slowly, the inevitability of it all begins to take hold. Tears well, and not just for me. Angie is still out there somewhere. What he's going through right now can only be imagined. At least he's not here, being forced to watch, and then probably take my place. At least he's not going to end up in a shallow grave somewhere out in the woods. He will live, for a while, but not in the world I could have given him. Once the money runs out, he'll most likely return to the street. No one will hunt him down. They won't have to. The street will kill him, this year or next, and when he's gone, alone and unnoticed, there will be no one left to remember either of us.

To hell with that! The only surrender that's happening here tonight is the one that fools them into thinking they've won. Whatever they plan to do to me, let them think the power is all theirs. That's when they'll grow careless. That's when they'll learn that a tiger in chains is still a tiger. One mistake, that's all; just one wrong move. So come on, boys, drink up because there's still a long time 'til dawn.

***

A hand clamps over my mouth, jerking me into alertness. There's a face close to mine. It takes me a moment to recognize it, and then some more moments to believe it. Somehow, impossibly, it's Angie. This can't be a dream because his hand is real. Those distant voices still drifting down the stairs are real.

Before removing the ball-gag, he raises a finger to his lips.

"Just get this damn thing off me, will you!" That bit comes out muffled, but he understands. Once it's done, the next bit comes out clear. "Oh my God: how? How did you find me?"

"I followed you."

"Followed? How could you have followed a speeding van?"

He grins broadly, at the same time looking ever so slightly smug as he releases me from the rest of my bonds. "I ran fast."

"Ran fast? What, like you swam all the way from Hawaii?"

He's smugger still. "Why not? Isn't that what heroes do? Besides, you learn to run fast when there's a cop chasing you. And they weren't speeding all the way. They made some turns, I cut across open ground and their taillights were the only ones out there. Now do you want a blow-by-blow account of how they didn't lock up behind them or do you wanna get dressed? Because we need to scram before they're done partying."

He's right, of course. It feels like Joey and the three creeps left hours ago. That's probably just me. There's waiting for them, and then there's almost going to sleep waiting for them. However long it's been, they must be just about ready by now. We have to leave, but not before Angie gets a hug so hard it could almost crush the breath out of him. "Thank God for you. I almost gave up. I almost believed I would never see you again."

"Hey, you started this, remember? You're not gonna get rid of me that easily. Now come on. Get dressed."

My clothes are strewn across the floor. Thanks, guys. You couldn't at least—then it hits me. "Wait a minute. You're talking. How in hell are you suddenly talking?"

He shrugs, the hoarseness of his newfound voice replying, "Dunno. Maybe it's a miracle. Now come on. We don't have time for this."

"A miracle, huh? Or you always could talk. You were simply refusing to."

His answer is another smirk. Well, enjoy it while you can, kid. We'll be coming back to this later. Right now though, he's right. We have to get out of here. Both the .38 and the 9mm are still inside our carryall. Chasing a speeding van must have made him forget to drop them. Still, as he watches me pull back the slide on the .38 and check its chamber, he lays his hand across it and shakes his head. "You promised. Remember?"

"Yes, I promised, but unless you're going to get us out of here as miraculously as you got in, I'm keeping this for plan

B, all right?" His face begins to wilt, like a kid who really needs that candy but isn't getting it. "Okay, okay, I promise I won't kill anyone, but there are still four jerks up there looking to fill some holes. I don't want to be one. I don't want to end up in one either. Do you?"

He doesn't, which is fortunate for Joey and his crew because, thanks to him, they will never know how lucky they just got. We creep up onto the main floor of the warehouse. Their voices get louder as we go. The van is still parked in the middle of it. Over to our left against the rear wall is a small office. That's where they've been drinking. They're done drinking now. Still cackling together as they step out, they're blissfully unaware of us watching them until they hear me shout, "The keys!"

All four of them stop. They look like a boy band whose fans just caught them in bed together.

"The keys! Throw me the keys to the van."

Joey flashes those teeth at me, almost like he was half expecting it. "Well now, aren't you the slippery one? They did say not to take you for granted. My mistake, huh? I guess we shoulda grabbed your friend here the same time we took you. So what's the plan then, sweet cheeks? If you were gonna shoot, you would've done it already."

"I only kill when I'm paid to. You know that because you're Network too, right?"

"That's right."

"And you were keeping tabs on me in New York. Why? For that matter, how? No one is supposed to know

126

where I live."

"We were worried about you. A couple of big hits like that. Who knows what a person might start thinking? They might start to get paranoid. They might start to think people were after them. So were we right or were we right? As to the how, you can figure that out for yourself, can't you?" He pauses, expecting me to actually try. If he's hoping that will distract me, he's wrong. "Your phone, sweet cheeks, your phone. We had your number, the one your texts came to, right up until you jumped that delivery van and smashed it. We've always known exactly where you were, right down to your apartment block. Hey, thanks for letting us know you were in St. Louis, by the way. We were beginning to think we might have to take you off our Christmas list."

While he's talking, he's signaling with his fingers. Driver and the other two creeps are starting to fan out. Really! He actually thinks he and his creeps are going to jump me.

"Oh, come on now. Why don't you put the gun down? You might take out one or two of us but then the rest of us will be really pissed. Or we could do a deal. I'll just tell 'em you got away. I'll make it sound really convincing. They'll believe me, what with you being so good at it anyway."

"But I am getting away."

The hammer drops and Joey goes down, clutching at his stomach as he cries, "Jesus Christ, the bitch just gut-shot me!"

Driver is next in my sights. "You know, if you don't get him to a vet, he's gonna bleed out. You will too if you don't throw me the keys, like now."

All three of them are standing with their hands slightly raised. Seeing them properly for the first time is something of a disappointment. These guys all look so boringly ordinary, just some average Joes no one would suspect of snatching kids off the street. Well, driver not so much. He's looking at me almost without expression, but it's a mask. The truth is right there in his eyes. If he had a weapon, he'd open up on both of us. The other two are not so sure.

With Joey squirming on the floor, clutching at the growing red patch on his stomach, they look to driver for a lead. He looks at them, stiffening as he sees they're not up for it. Now there's anger in his eyes, a cold fury at having been taken so easily. Not yet quite ready to submit, he needs a little more encouragement.

"Your choice, creep. I can leave all of you gut-shot if you like. You'll probably bleed out together before anyone finds you."

A moment more of pure hate and he reaches into his pants pocket, takes out the keys, and throws them at us. Angie takes possession of them. He needs no second telling. While he fires up the van, with me backing away toward the passenger's side, driver calls out, "See you soon, honey. Maybe next time we'll make a snuff movie together."

"Oh, I can't wait. Sounds like a role to die for. You'll be the perfect lead."

If driver has an answer, it's lost in the revving of the engine and the squealing of tires as Angie crashes us backward through the doors and out into the street. Driving who knows where on the lamplit streets of a city neither of us has been to before, eventually we come to a piece of wasteland next to some railroad tracks. The other three sides are masked by scrubby trees and we park close up in the corner nearest the road. For now, we should be safe. Driver and the two creeps will be too busy dealing with Joey to come after us immediately. For what's left of the night, we try to get some sleep.

CHAPTER ELEVEN

C ome the morning, with the sun fully risen, we abandon the van. We could drive it to Oklahoma City, but that's not a risk worth taking. Driver made it plain he wasn't done with us and he'll certainly recognize his own snatch wagon. He'll recognize me too, and most likely Angie, unless we change things up. We need to go shopping.

As for getting out of Kansas, my St. Louis plan is still good: an internet café, pay and pick up tickets to Oklahoma City, then buy tickets to Portland at the bus station.

First of all though, we haven't eaten since leaving the collective. Nor have we been able to freshen up, and one of us at least feels a pressing need to wash off some of last night's filth. There's a bar and grill within sight of the railroad tracks. We walk on over, leaving the .38 in the van. If the authorities ever connect it to the body in the woods, it'll be driver and the two creeps who have some questions to answer.

Angie goes to the washroom, leaving me to order breakfast: eggs Benedict and coffee. It arrives at the same time as he returns. While we eat, the silence that settles between us becomes ever more pregnant. Once again, this needs to be dealt with quickly. "What's wrong, babe?"

His only answer is a shrug, which is becoming a tad annoying. This pretense of you not being able to talk is over, and we will be getting to that later. So come on, talk to me.

"It's last night, isn't it? Look, I know you don't like violence, but you know I had to. Those creeps were going to put both of us in a shallow grave; and I didn't kill him, just like I promised, even though he deserved it. They all did."

"Did they? None of them had guns. We could've just taken the van and driven away."

"Could we? You were there. Do you really think they were just going to let us leave?"

"You're right. I was there. Two of them weren't going to do anything."

"And I didn't shoot them. They were followers, harmless. The other two weren't. They were dangerous. They probably got their kicks from the killings, not the rapes. So I shot one of them and gave the other one a reason to think twice. Besides, if I hadn't shot one of them, they would have come straight after us. The one with the keys made that perfectly clear. So I gave them something to keep them busy as well, busy enough hopefully so that we can quit Kansas City before they come looking for us."

He looks away, not quite able to square the necessity of it with his distaste for it. Poor thing. The urge to hug him is strong, but he ceased being a puppy some time ago—

or a daughter, for that matter. Hugs and feels will not cut it anymore. He wants something more, something that may be impossible for me to give. "I still think you shoot people too easily. And what's this Network you called that guy out on?"

"Network?"

"Yeah. Network. You said he was Network too. So what is this Network that both of you are part of?"

There's a storm brewing again, not quite as bad as on that road before St. Louis, but still, this is something we do not need to be talking about right now.

"It's a group of people I used to be in with. We had a falling out, and they're not very forgiving."

"A falling out! You call what they were planning to do a falling out? Man, I'd hate to see what happens when you really piss someone off. So what did you do, rat them out or something and that's why we're on the run?"

"No. If anything, they ratted me out, and we're on the run because of that guy on the High Line. You know that. Look, I know this is hard for you, but I'm not some psycho serial killer. I'm just trying to keep us safe, exactly as I said I would. If you don't believe that, why did you come for me? You had a bag full of money, a new ID, and a couple of guns. You could've just walked away and been free of me."

"I couldn't do that. I'm your angel, remember?"

"Wow. I'm getting goosebumps all over. Not only are you my very own personal hero, you're my angel too. All you gotta do now is learn to fly." He laughs because that's ridiculous. Well, good. That's what he's supposed to think. "It's you and me together, babe: Monster Mom and Angel. We got our superpowers rockin' and they can't handle it."

"Oh, man." More laughter; which is also good since it stops him asking any more questions about the Network. "Okay, you're forgiven. So what do we do now?"

"Now? Now we go shopping. I know how much you enjoy that."

"Yeah."

Aww, poor thing. Well, suck it up, kid, because it is what it is. Leaving him to deal with that, it's my turn to hit the washroom. Then there's just the bill to pay with a big, buttering-up tip for the lady who served us.

"Could you help us? This is our first time in Kansas City and we need a change of clothes. We've been thumbing for a while and you probably noticed these are getting a little stale. Where would be the place to go for that?"

She noticed all right. When we first walked in, she looked at us like we were a couple of bums who might just dirty up the place. Now she's all smiles and wouldn't doubt us for a second. "Well, here in KC, River Market is where you go. They got everything there you could possibly need. I'll call you a cab, if you like."

"That would be great. Thank you so much."

The ride is short. As the cab pulls away, we are left looking up at an arch. It says we're about to enter the historic City Market. Well, great. River Market and City Market are the exact same place, and this is the exact same spot Joey snatched me from. A quick glance around reveals no sign of driver and the two creeps. Maybe they're still dealing with Joey. That's a doubtful assumption. Even for geniuses like them, a shallow grave doesn't take that long to dig; but maybe the ride there and back does. Either way, standing around here isn't getting anything done.

The shopping is as good as promised, and soon enough we have everything we need. There's a simple, blue dress with a short coat and a shoulder-length blonde wig for me, some makeup, and the biggest pair of sunglasses on offer. For Angie, there's a suit and some shears because that hair has got to go. We find somewhere secluded to change and he gets a buzz cut. It's a shame, but it has to be. With his hair tied back, he could have passed for some incognito rock star. Never mind. He's still all teenage sex on legs: *my* teenage sex on legs.

To the rest of the world, we probably look like some old rich guy thought he was still in his thirties. We got married and he stayed alive just long enough for me to have his kid and take his money. Somewhere out there is an entire family who would hire a hitman if they could afford to. Well, suck it up, shmucks. You got the class; we got the inheritance.

All blonded up, we set out in search of an internet cafe and book tickets to Oklahoma City. Our bus leaves at 1:00 p.m. There's time enough for us to have an early lunch. We find a place, farm to table. With its wood flooring and rustic furniture, it's nice. It's also busy, but loud, pushy, and loaded has no trouble talking her way in. She also attracts some unwanted attention, or maybe it's Angie, because some of the ladies do seem just a little bit too interested. He's my son, okay? Fussed over throughout our meal of red pepper ricotta dips and albondigas because there's none of you getting your hands on him today.

With lunch over, we should probably be heading straight for the bus station. As we step out onto the sidewalk though, who should be walking toward us but driver. He's looking a little lost, like a guy who doesn't need directions. He just knows how to get there, y'know? Apart from that, he's just a face in the crowd. We could be too, except, even as my sunglasses are slipped on, he sees me looking. Taking that as an open invitation, he heads straight for us. Great! And we almost made it out clean too.

"Excuse me, ma'am. You wouldn't happen to have seen two kids hanging around, would you? They'd be wearing hoodies and sweatpants. They're my boys, and they didn't come home last night."

He hasn't recognized us yet. Brazening it out should keep it that way, what with me already being dressed for the part.

"Oh, wow. I'm really sorry to hear that. But ain't that just kids, huh? Always disappearing and getting into trouble. I swear you gotta watch 'em every minute of every day. Oh, I'm sorry. Where are my manners? This here is my boy. Isn't he just such a cutie? I love him to bits, y'know? God help me for all the trouble he's put me through. Still, I would hate for him to disappear like that. Have you been to the cops yet, for all the good they ever do? 'Ah, they're probably just gettin' into mischief somewhere. Give us a call if they ain't back by this time tomorrow.' And this is what we pay taxes for, right?"

"Er, yeah, I guess." Just for an instant, he's looking a little dazed. "Anyway, I thought I'd look myself, y'know? It's probably no biggie. They're just up to mischief, like you said."

"Yeah. What a pity they can't be more like girls, huh? Mind you, the stories I could tell you about my sister's girl. I swear, one of these days she'll give her father a heart attack, the poor bastard. But hey, what can you do? Just hope they don't get knocked up by some punk so you get stuck with a punk son-in-law, or he just disappears and leaves us holding the baby. My God, if I'd ever done something like that my father would've given me such a beating. But that's kids these days, right? They think everything's a free lunch."

"Ain't that the truth? Well, you have a good day now."

"Hey, you too. And I hope you find your boys."

Battered into submission or because he's made us, he hurries away. For sure, he's not wasting time bothering anyone else as he leaves. Some fluff has suddenly and very conveniently appeared on Angie's lapel. Brushing it off allows me to keep an eye on him every step of the way. Before turning a corner, he gives us the quickest look back. Maybe we're busted; maybe not. It doesn't matter because time is running down. We have a bus to catch and a cab to find before that.

***

The bus station is a red brick block on the outside, with sterile tiles on the inside, and a lot of bored people standing around or sitting on hard seating. At least the line for tickets is short. This is good because as soon as we walk in there's some guy having his luggage searched. The two very business-like gentlemen doing it just have to be undercover cops. They must think he's a drug mule or something. That changes my plan instantly.

We were going to buy tickets in sweatpants and hoodies, just two brothers travelling together, but we have an illegal firearm in our carryall. The last thing we need is the law taking an interest. We buy tickets as mom and son instead, then slip out before the cops can even begin to suspect they've just missed the biggest arrest of their careers.

Changing behind some parked buses in a corner of the lot, we catch our ride to Oklahoma City. It leaves more or less on time and we settle in, way up back and minding our own business. As the wheels beneath us eat up the road and the hours, we catch up on some sleep until late afternoon brings us into Wichita. There, as we stretch our legs, Angie nods toward a car that's just purred into an adjacent parking lot. "I think that's following us."

"Yeah. Why?"

"Because it was there in Lawrence, and then there it was again in Topeka."

The car sits black and brooding, its occupants hidden behind smoked glass. It could be anybody, but Angie has no doubt.

"Looks like that guy in Kansas City meant what he said. Unless there's somebody else you ratted out as well."

"I already told you. They ratted me out."

The Deep Web should be on its way to Portland. If the Network is in its pocket, so should they. That leaves driver and the two creeps. He must have made us and now here they are looking for some payback. Or Angie's got it wrong. He certainly doesn't think so, not with that big, fat smirk on his face like he's suddenly figured it all out.

"Whatever. At least we know someone is on us."

"What do you mean by that?"

"Oh, come on. You gotta admit. Doesn't exactly feel like we're running from the law, does it? I mean, that state trooper after Harrisburg. All he was about was you dumping me on the side of the road. And the hotel in St. Louis. You don't know for sure why the cops were there. Like that guy in the crowd said. It could've been a stiff."

"Or a fugitive they've been after for a while. Just because you don't see them, don't mean they're not there. Besides, it's a big country. Outside of the major cities, it's not that easy to find someone unless they're stupid."

"And you're not, are you." He's becoming more challenging by the moment. "Okay. If you're wanted so bad, why is no one tagging us? I was there when those cops came to your apartment. They said they'd been called to a noise disturbance. You said it was about some guy you capped on the High Line. Dumb ain't stupid but maybe, you'd prefer it if it was."

The way this conversation is going, you in a dress and being difficult was preferable. That was a walk in the park compared to this increasingly confident young man who's started asking way too many searching questions.

"You still think I'm lying to you?"

He's not smirking anymore. He's looking me straight in the eye. "I've seen you lie to everyone we've met. I've seen you change identity like, well, like you change ID. Whoever you wanna be, you are, so long as it gets you what you want. So tell me you're not faking out on me too. Tell me you're not just stringing me along."

"Why would I do that? This is you and me together now and I've told you more truth than you've ever told me. But, if you really wanna go there, it's quid pro quo, baby. You want me to tell you something you think I'm keeping from you, well then you gotta start telling me what you're keeping from me. Like, for instance, why are you talking, and why weren't you talking before? How about we start with that?"

Instead, he laughs, short and cynical. "And there you go again, throwing it all back on me. You think I don't see you doing that? Every time you're challenged it's like, yeah, but what about you? Well not this time, baby, not this time!"

He walks away, leaving me wordless and hanging. Yeah, you in a dress was definitely preferable. At least we both knew who was in control. But then, maybe he's right. Maybe that's my problem. Being in control for so long has become a habit. It's not just his voice that's been getting stronger since Kansas City. He is too, becoming his own person right there in front of me and here's me not knowing how to give him the space. On the other hand, he's not the adult here. He's not paying for it all. He doesn't get to make judgments like that.

This is getting complicated again.

All of this will have to wait though. Our bus is about to leave. The car continues to sit there brooding, with no one stepping out. If it is driver and the two creeps, enjoy the ride, guys, because we both know you can't touch us until Oklahoma City.

***

The bus pulls in around mid-evening. Despite sleeping a good deal of the way, we are both too tired to do anything more than find a room for the night. As we step out of the bus station, we search for the car. It's nowhere to be seen, but that doesn't mean a thing. If the Jayhawks are following us, they must have a plan. It's probably not a very good plan because dumbasses don't need good plans. They just need something to shoot at. Since they're not shooting at us yet, we disappear around back of the bus station and change: me into my only dress and blonde wig, he into his suit. Two boys may have gotten off the bus but it's a mom and her son who walk down the road to a nearby motel.

Safe within our room, we shower. Angie goes first. He's in and out like a guy. My turn is a luxurious wallow, all soap and steam and the cleaning away of the last twenty-four hours. If it had been a bath, there would have been candles and wine and all the time in the world. That mood ends when all this scented gorgeousness wrapped only in a towel is ignored. He's sitting on the edge of the bed staring at the floor. This is ominous. Maybe he's ready to open up to me at last. If so, this has to be handled carefully. Neither of us needs another scene like St. Louis.

"Hey, baby. You okay?"

He brightens up a little at the touch of my hand.

"Yeah, I was just thinking is all. Those guys meant to kill us back there in Kansas City, didn't they? Not that I'm letting you off your promise or anything, but you were right to do what you did. If they are the ones following us now, maybe you should've shot the rest of them too."

"Wow! Look at you. Quite the regular wise guy all of a sudden. Hey, don't you worry about those jerks. They got nothing they're gonna surprise me with. And as for shooting them back in Kansas, I know you don't mean that. You're far too good a person to be thinking like that. I might even call you my better half. Hell, if you keep this up, you might even make an honest citizen out of me. I mean, wow, the world turned on its head, right?"

That gets a laugh out of him. Okay, maybe this isn't that conversation, but it will do.

"Because you love me, right? Well, maybe I love you too. You know, maybe. It's possible."

"Aww, sweetie, look at you. You're blushing and everything." He is now anyway. "Aww, come here. Mommy wants to kiss her little soldier all over."

Pulled in and assaulted with big kisses, he tries to pull away, but only half-heartedly. "Get off me, will you? Shit, man! I'm supposed to be your hero, not your baby. Heroes don't get their faces washed in Mommy's spit."

"Oh, I'm sorry. Mommy just plain forgot you're all grown up now. Besides, how do you know heroes don't get their faces washed in Mommy's spit? You ever meet a hero's mom? I bet they all grew up on apple pie and spit washes."

"Yeah, right. Like—"

A loud rapping at the door shatters the moment.

"Police! Open up!"

Shit! Great timing, guys. There must be an entire section in the training manual on how to turn up at precisely the wrong moment. As to why they're here, there isn't time to ask as the hammering becomes louder and even more insistent. "Police! Open up now!"

"Okay! Okay! I'm coming! I'm coming!"

The door opens on two officers, both female. They do not look at all happy, but then who would wearing those uniforms? While the second one stands back, scowling like it's an Olympic sport, door abuser says, "We have reason to believe you have a minor in there with you."

"A minor? Well, yes, I have my son in here with me."

"Your son." She looks me up and down.

"Yes. I was just taking a shower."

My towel is still firmly in place. My expression is all innocent and confused. There's nothing unseemly going on here, Officer, as God is my witness. But she's not buying it.

"Stand aside, ma'am!"

They stalk into the room. Two evangelists entering a whore house couldn't be more disapproving. Angie, still sitting on the edge of the bed, has had the good sense to throw on some clothes. Door abuser glances around the room, then looks him over. "So this is your son, huh? You have some ID?"

Indeed we do, and now we're about to find out just how good Ray's work is. She inspects them closely—very closely. It's impossible to tell whether she's buying them or not. She hands them to her partner. She also inspects them, very closely.

"You had his hair cut," says door abuser. "Why'd you have his hair cut?"

"Because it was time. You know how it is when they grow out of something. At least he didn't decide he wanted to have a tattoo."

No, she doesn't know how it is. "You'll be coming with us. Now get dressed, unless you wanna be taken out of here in a towel."

CHAPTER TWELVE

This is an interview room somewhere downtown: sterile, impersonal, brightly lit, and worn down at the corners. The OCPD has me under the Mann Act: that's transporting a minor across state lines. Someone dropped a dime on us. Could've been the clerk at the motel, but that doesn't seem very likely. He had no reason to think we were anything other than a mom and son. That only leaves the Jayhawks. Well, credit where credit's due. Turns out driver has some smarts after all. Why go to all the risk of taking revenge himself when he could just turn me over to the state of Oklahoma and watch me go down for maybe ten years? Except, of course, it won't be the state of Oklahoma and it won't be ten years.

Angie is somewhere else. That complicates matters, but never mind. They've left me sitting here for at least an hour, so this must be where they let me sweat. Sorry, guys. There's a building full of cops to figure a way out of before they pick up on that outstanding warrant in New York, and before the Deep Web picks up on the prize package just sitting here all gift-wrapped and tied up in a bow.

The door opens. Two detectives walk in. They're both female. That could be a blessing or a curse. One of them is caramel blonde, tightly tied back. She's dressed like Oklahoma City just got hit by the worst fashion drought in history. All of it screams I'm better than any man and, if I have to, I'll work eighteen hours a day to prove it; or maybe I just like working eighteen hours a day. The other one's a dark brunette, except for the rainbow highlights. She looks like she just finished a shift undercover, or maybe she just likes street punk chic and cheap jewelry. They sit down opposite me, as businesslike as the jacket they dump in front of me.

"Hey," says caramel. "Busy night, huh?"

Highlights stares at me, the queen bee who wants to know why the hell I'm sitting at the same table as her. You run with it, honey. You're playing right into my hands as scared little me says to caramel, "Am I under arrest?"

"Not yet." She flicks open the jacket. "But you've got some serious explaining to do. So, let's see what we've got then, shall we? One carryall, containing two fake IDs, a thousand dollars or thereabouts in new bills, a few items of clothing, and a firearm. We're still checking but I'll take a guess it's not registered. Seems to me you must've left somewhere in quite a hurry. And then there's the boy, not above sixteen, by the looks of him. Quiet kid, doesn't say a lot. Well, nothing at all, really. You say he's your son. Somehow, I think a DNA test might say different. Anything you'd like to say at this point?"

Yes. Thank God we lost that other carryall in St. Louis. Otherwise, this would be a whole different ball game. As it is, they think they've got it sewn up: woman kidnaps boy for sex romp across Midwest. Except it ain't always what it looks like, especially once it's been spun for all it's worth.

"Look. I'm sorry. Really, I am. God, I must have broken so many laws; but you don't understand. You're right; he's not my son. He's my neighbor's son. I moved into a new apartment a few months ago. Everything was fine at first, but then I began to see him in the hallway. He was always so sad, always avoiding looking at me. And he was so thin, like he wasn't eating properly. I just knew something was wrong. I know. I shouldn't have interfered. I should've just called the authorities, but I felt so sorry for him. I got him into my apartment. I fed him. I tried to get him talking for a week or more, and I thought I was getting there. And then . . . well, then . . ."

Caramel and highlights exchange a glance. They're beginning to figure it out, just like they're meant to. Now it's time to go in for the kill.

"And then his father came. There was the hammering at the door, and the big voice demanding to be let in. I knew who it was. I could see the boy shaking with fear. I tried to tell him to go away but he just busted his way in. 'What the hell you think you're doin', lady?' he says. 'Stay the eff away from my kid.' I tried to stop him. But what could I do? After that, he starts harassing me. I don't know what to do. If I report it, it's just bad neighbors, right? Keep out of his way, or find another apartment. Then the boy goes missing. I don't know. Maybe he's hiding or something. The big bully comes straight to me, forces his way in and accuses me of hiding him. This time, I try to fight back but he's too big, too strong. I can't stop him. I just can't stop him from . . ."

My voice has dropped to almost a whisper. Caramel is sitting forward in her chair. Highlights is on the edge of something too. If bully was here right now, my money would be on her.

"What?" says caramel. "What couldn't you stop him from doing?"

My eyes are tear-filled, my nose is all sniffly, but the words have to be said, the unnamable has to be named. "He raped me. I just couldn't stop him. And then he tells me if I ever say a word to anyone, he'll kill me. Or maybe he'll just say his son raped me too. His own son! How could anyone do that to their own child? I knew I couldn't stay there any longer. I mean, what was to stop him from coming back anytime he wanted? I couldn't just leave the boy there either, not with a brute like that. So I got the IDs and the gun. I scraped together as much money as I could and, the first time I saw him again, I just took the boy and ran. And that's the truth. I swear it. Please, you have to believe me. Why would I lie?"

My pleading is little more than window dressing at this point. The door is open. It just has to be walked through.

"And that's why the boy hardly talks, is it?" says highlights. "Because of the abuse."

"Yes." Damn! That's the cherry on top and she saw it before me. "Yes, he hardly ever says a word. It must be because of the beatings, and then what that man did to me. Please, you must let us go. I know he's coming after us. If he finds us, he'll kill us. You can't let him find us."

Caramel reaches out a reassuring hand. "You're in a building full of police officers, ma'am. We serve with pride. That's what it says on the side of our vehicles. So if he is coming after you, there's no way he's going to get to you in here. Now, you just sit tight and we'll be back. Okay?"

"Okay. And thank you."

They leave, with even highlights looking more sympathetic. It's not a done deal yet though. They must have a superior to talk to, with the fake IDs and firearm still to be answered for. Those they could book me for right now. If they do, if they put my face on the system, it's all over. The Deep Web will be here within an hour. Sitting here waiting for them isn't an option, but then neither is anything else. From simply walking out, a non-starter if ever there was one, through taking hostage the officer they send in to babysit me, a bonehead move, to throwing a panic attack, which might lead to sedatives and being cuffed to a bed, each one is worse than the last, and none of them will get Angie out.

Fortunately, before desperation can force me into actually trying one of them, caramel returns. Jacket again in hand as she sits down opposite me, she's just as businesslike as before. "Okay. There are some quite serious charges here but, in light of possible extenuating circumstances, the chief has decided we're not going to charge you at this time. We have procedures we have to follow, especially where an accusation of rape is concerned. Since you're not under arrest, we can't hold you in the cells. We are, however, still concerned for your safety, so we're going to put you up in a hotel with a couple of detectives to watch over you. There are still some questions you're going to have to answer though, starting with a name and address. Who's the boy's father and where does he live?"

They already know the names we were brought in under are fake. Now they're on board with my rape story, they're not going to suspect our new names are fake as well. Mine is the ID for one of my accommodation addresses in New York. It's a brownstone apartment block in a rundown part of town, just the kind of place where you might expect to find a thug. Angie gets the surname of one of the other tenants. His name is right there by the front door. We've never met. We never will. Caramel will figure out she's been fed a line soon enough.

"Okay. Now about the IDs and the firearm. Where did you get them?"

"A friend of a friend. It's that kind of neighborhood. You just have to know the right people and have the cash." She doesn't like that answer. "He's a friend, okay? I don't want to get him into trouble. He was helping us. That's gotta count for something."

149

Or not. She stands up. "We'll deal with that tomorrow. When we contact the NYPD, they're gonna want a name. It's not just us who could press charges, you know, so perhaps you ought to sleep on it. For now, we need to get you to a hotel."

Waiting for us in the lobby is Angie. My relief at seeing him is real; my gratitude to the OCPD entirely fake. As for naming names, we won't be sticking around long enough for that, especially when they introduce us to the two detectives who are going to watch over us. They're a curious pairing. He is overweight, pasty, balding, and probably not far from retirement. She is thin, careworn, and looks like she'd have trouble saying boo to a goose. Their chief must have thought it was time they got out from behind a desk. They're babysitting a scared woman and a traumatized boy, people, not some mobster who's turned state's evidence.

As our car slides out onto the street, there's no sign of the Jayhawks. If they're here, they're keeping a low profile. Hopefully it stays that way, because there's no way these two over-the-hill detectives are going to stop them.

Through downtown they drive us, street lights and nightcrawlers: pretty girls in short-short dresses and pretty boys in tight-tight pants. But for driver, that could have been Angie and me. Instead, for us, time is running out: drip, drip, drip. Never mind. This game isn't over yet. There are still moves to be made.

On the plus side, we are no longer in a building full of cops. There are only these two to deal with. On the minus side, our carryall hasn't come with us. We are without money, ID, guns, transport, or even a change of clothes. Then again, that female detective does look to be about the same size as me.

***

The hotel is out on the west side, close to an intersection, an easy escape route. We have a suite. It's quite reasonable, really, considering the OCPD is paying for it. If it wasn't for that and the two detectives, this would've done us very well for the night. As it is, they sit in the living room while we sit in the bedroom. That suits me fine. Until an opportunity presents itself, the illusion is all that matters. We are poor, helpless victims and they are here to protect us.

Time drags slowly by. Occasionally, just to help the illusion along, restless anxiety forces me to wander in and out. Seeing my unease, they are happy to respond to my fitful conversation with calming words. It's a shame, really. They seem like genuinely nice people, but there's still a professional in here. At any moment, they might receive a call and all my lies will be laid bare. When that moment comes, if it comes, there will be no room for sentimentality in what follows.

At last, my opportunity arrives. The female detective stands, excuses herself, and makes for the bathroom. The cable is ripped from the bedside phone and coiled into a garrote. The other detective is sitting facing me, but takes no notice of my nervous busyness. He's used to it by now. Time no longer drags. It's short and growing shorter. Out of his line of sight, the garrote drops quickly over his head. He begins to struggle, clawing first at the cable and then trying for me, but he can't reach. While he kicks and flails, Angie watches like the living embodiment of a conscience only he has any use for right now. Get over it, kid. This is no time for squeamishness.

Once the detective has weakened enough, he's pushed to the floor, red-faced and gasping. That's a little troubling, but it's way too late to start worrying about a heart attack. His gun is mine; his cuffs are thrown to Angie. Still in the grip of his righteous disapproval, he hesitates to use them. Even a hard stare from me does not move him.

From the bathroom comes the sound of flushing. There are only seconds before she appears. We don't have time for this. "Do it, for chrissakes!"

The door opens. She steps out. The muzzle of her partner's firearm presses into her temple. She freezes. "What the hell? What are you doing?"

"I'm checking out. Now strip."

She does not obey. Maybe she's wasting time, looking for an angle, trying to be the cop she once was. The gun presses harder into her temple. "Look at your partner, Detective. I don't want to hurt you but if I have to, I will. Now strip!"

She looks. Her partner isn't moving at all. Well, if he has had a heart attack, they'll just have to add it to the list. She also looks at Angie. He stands like a vegan outside a steak house; to me, the coolly simmering outrage that might explode with indignation at any moment, just like in St. Louis. To her, he must look like a cold-blooded killer, a psycho who might do unspeakable things if someone wasn't there to control him. It's enough to persuade her. "Okay, okay."

We take not just her clothes but her firearm, both their badges, and whatever money we can find, leaving them cuffed and gagged on the floor. Thanks to the Jayhawks, OK City has been something of a ride. They're still out there, but for now, we're OK too, and it's hard to resist the parting shot. "Don't forget to say a big thank you to all the guys down at the precinct. Really, you've been so generous it makes me feel all warm inside."

Angie isn't at all amused.

***

It's past 2:00 a.m. No one sees us leave. If we're lucky, our ex-protectors won't be found until morning. In the parking lot, the detective's clothes—black pants, white blouse, and a houndstooth jacket—turn out to be a little tight. Never mind. There are more important things to think about. We have guns. We have transport. We have a little over a hundred dollars. We have a head start, and there's still no sign of the Jayhawks.

Heading west into the night, after about fifteen minutes it occurs to me this vehicle probably has a tracker on it.

The parking lot of a supercenter in Mustang is as good as a dealership's forecourt. There are a number of vehicles dotted around. We park up next to one and wait, then wait, and wait. Just when it's beginning to look like we may have to steal one, somebody appears. He's some dude, with a mullet and a beard. Nothing unusual about that except this guy is wearing a white tutu with a fluffy skirt down to his knees and tiny fairy wings on his back. Beneath the skirt his thin, hairy legs reach all the way down to a pair of ballet pumps. Carrying two cartons of beer; that must be some party he's come out to resupply. It's hardly for me to judge, but maybe he's been drinking. Perhaps he drove here after hours of it. No one wants a DUI on their record. This shouldn't be too difficult.

"Excuse me, sir."

My stolen badge flashes in the parking lot lights. Dude looks at it, underwhelmed to the point of boredom.

"Really? A princess can't make a beer run at three in the morning without being hassled by you people?"

"You can do whatever you want so long as you're doing it with adults. I'm more interested in whether you've been drinking before you drove here tonight."

"And this is Bring Your Son to Work Day too, is it?"

That's hardly fair. Angie's doing the best he can, but then it doesn't really matter. We're close enough for my badge to be replaced with a gun. "Put the beer down! Do as you're told and you won't get hurt."

"Now, you see, I've been busted before. I know how real cops do it."

"Great. Now put the beer down and give him your keys."

He shakes his head, puts the beer down, and reaches for his keys. "Lady, if you want the car so bad, all you had to do was ask. Just don't forget to torch it when you're done. The insurance company owes me an upgrade by now."

"Well, I'm sure I'll be happy to oblige. Now move."

While Angie takes possession of his car, dude walks in front of me toward ours. So far, no one else has come out of the supercenter. No one inside appears to have noticed. All we need to do is stow this one for a few hours.

"Open the trunk."

"Aww, hell. You don't have to do that. I'd be happy to just sit here and drink my beer for, say, fifteen minutes. Then I'll call my friends to come pick me up. I won't even call the real cops until tomorrow morning. Now doesn't that sound like a plan to you?"

"Possibly. So what guarantee do I have—"

A car screams into the parking lot and screeches to a halt maybe fifty feet from us. It's black, brooding, and instantly recognizable. The Jayhawks have come looking for their showdown.

CHAPTER THIRTEEN

"Hey, bitch!" yells driver as the three of them leap out of their vehicle, all of them packing AR-15s.

Dude is already running, his thin legs pumping beneath his flouncing skirt, his wings flapping uselessly behind him. No one cares. Angie is calling for me to get into his car, but that ain't happening. This has to be dealt with, right here, right now.

"Leave. Wait for me down the road."

He refuses. A burst of fire has me diving behind the police vehicle. Angie doesn't get it. He's a sitting duck. This time some frantic signaling makes him understand, and at last he goes. More fire follows. It rips straight through the police vehicle, showering glass all around. Belly-down amongst it, my view of them from underneath the vehicle is clear, as clear as their naively simple plan. They mean to flank me on both sides. What a shame they're such amateurs. You've got no cover, guys. You're going down.

"See, bitch!" cries driver. "I told you we'd be seeing you again, but don't worry. We ain't gonna put you in a snuff movie. The kid'll do just fine for that. You'd be surprised how much some people will pay to watch a little piggyback action with extra added butchery for dessert."

Not as surprised as you're about to be. The two detectives' firearms have only the ammunition in their mags. It will have to do. More fire rips through the police vehicle. In the pause that follows, I'm up on my feet and the one to my right has an entire mag emptied at him. He goes down. Wounded or dead, no one cares because already in the distance we can hear sirens. We have a minute, tops.

Driver and the other Jayhawk are backing away. They don't want to get caught. Me neither, but with only one mag left, downed guy's AR-15 has become a necessity.

Darting toward it draws a few more token rounds. After that, they're piling into their car and, AR-15 in hand, my feet are pounding for the exit Angie left by. Out onto a side street and he's beside me.

"Drive! Just drive!"

We're running west on the 152. Less than a minute behind us are the Jayhawks. Behind them, after they've figured it out, will be who knows how many cops. The road stretches straight ahead of us for a couple of minutes through suburbs. This still has to be settled, tonight, but not until we're out in the country.

The suburbs end, first to our right and then to our left. There are still isolated properties, but the people inside must all be sleeping. By the time they've woken up and realized what's going down, it will all be over.

At my urging, Angie pulls over into the scrubland on the other side of the road. There's a high, boarded fence opposite. This is as good a place as any for an ambush.

"Take this!" The still-loaded firearm is thrust at him, but he refuses to take it. "Look, I know you don't like this, but they mean to kill us. You wanna be raped and slaughtered on the Dark Web for the entertainment of a bunch of rich guys while their kids are asleep upstairs? Take it!"

Again, he doesn't.

"All you've gotta do is back me up. That's all. You just gotta look like you mean it. I'll do the rest. Now, for chrissakes, take it!"

At last, he does. His face is hidden in darkness, but his distaste is almost palpable. Sorry, kid, but sometimes you just gotta do what has to be done.

We get out of the car and hunker down just behind the driver's side rear lights. They won't see us until it's too late. How much is left in the AR-15 is guesswork, but downed guy didn't get off that many shots. It will have to be enough.

We wait for their headlights to appear in the distance. It is them. It has to be them. No one else could be powering toward us on this road like that. If it's not them—well then it's collateral damage, baby, the fog of war. They sure as hell look like the enemy to me.

Their headlights bear down on us. The AR-15 sputters into the void above them. Their engine roars. Their tires squeal. The car swerves and flips, rolling over and over through the fence and into the property beyond. We should leave, but now the AR-15 needs more ammo. Telling Angie to get our car back on the road, I head for theirs.

It's belly-up, a steaming wreck. The smell of leaking gas is all around me, but the Jayhawks are both dead. There's another AR-15 between them but it's caught on something. It won't come free. There are lights going on in the house. The mag is enough. There's also a bag hanging down between them. It won't come free either but there are three more mags inside. Looks like these fools were expecting a small war. Aww, you guys. You're just making me feel so, y'know . . .

Back across the road, Angie is waiting with the passenger's side door already open. It's barely shut before his foot hits the gas. However far behind us the cops might be, some of them at least are going to have to stop and deal with that.

Straight west on the 152 and we're coming up on Union City. A little before it, we come upon an auto shop. It's nearly 4:00 a.m. The place is deserted. We park out of sight of the highway. Any moment now, we should hear sirens screaming by. They'll be looking for us in Union City. Then they'll be setting up checkpoints. We need to be a long way from here as soon as possible, with a new vehicle. Where better than this auto shop—

"You want quid pro quo?" His voice comes out of the silence like a lamentation for the world. "Well, here's my truth. It was what, seven years ago. My parents took me to the mall. It was a Saturday afternoon. There were lots of people around. They were just out living the dream: all you can eat and all you can buy. Then I see this man walk in. He's nothing special, just some guy—until he pulls out a couple of guns and starts killing people. No reason for it. Just one of those days, y'know? My parents tried to run. He took them both out. The last thing they ever did was cover me. That's how I survived. He just didn't see me lying there beneath them. I don't even know who he was. I've never wanted to. All I remember of him are those dead eyes."

There in the darkness, it's not his words that are striking at my heart and clawing at my throat. It's the monotone with which they are delivered, the complete lack of emotion. Oh, Angie, you should be screaming at the world. You should be raging at the careless injustice of it. Instead, your answer was an inconsolable sorrow. Mine was a simmering desire to hurt my parents as they hurt me. Your parents died because it was Saturday; mine because my need went too far.

Suddenly, and for the first time in twenty years, there is shame in that, and tears begin to well because, compared to him, my own cherished victimhood suddenly seems self-indulgent, self-centered; even arrogant.

"Anyway, security finally showed up and shot the guy dead. Afterward, they tried to talk to me but I wouldn't talk to them. Why should I? What did they know, and what was I supposed to say, anyway? Some guy just walked into a mall and shot my parents because . . . why not? Shit happens, right? Eventually, they just gave up. I don't blame them for that. I wasn't exactly helping. As for the rest of it, it wasn't so bad. I learned how the world really is. I survived. What else can anyone do?"

"Oh, baby." He doesn't resist being taken into my arms. There's not even a hint that he's looking for sympathy. Shit happens, right? Either you deal with it or it destroys you.

He is not destroyed. He's not even angry. "I don't blame you for killing those guys. You had to do it. I guess I'm not such a wise guy after all."

The darkness is silent. If our ghosts are out there watching they turn away, allowing us some moments in which to share the sorrow that's now mine as well as his. Then a whole flock of sirens goes screaming by out on the highway and necessity forces us to get moving. "Come on, baby. Let's go find a new car."

We break into the shop through a window. No alarms go off, unless there's a silent one. Inside, we find auto heaven: a treasure trove of vehicles all packed in bumper-to-bumper like a klotski puzzle waiting to be solved. There's no time to waste on being choosey. The one directly in front of the sectional door is sleek and sporty. It will do.

In the office, we find the keys. There's also a windbreaker that can be put to good use. So far, so good. What happens next is called look like you have a plan even though you don't until some bankers boxes stacked against a wall gives me a light bulb moment. By the time we leave, Angie is on the floor between the rear and front seats with a whole lot of those boxes stacked on top of him. He's not too happy about it, but he just gets a good shushing for his trouble.

This plan is barefaced cheek. Don't ruin it by complaining at the wrong moment.

No fugitive would be stupid enough to return to the mayhem they just caused, right? So we head back toward Mustang. Sure enough, there are the authorities dealing with the overturned wreck, and a none-too-happy homeowner. A cop waves us down. If he asks for documents, my foot will be hitting the gas and to hell with it. The window slides down and he places a hand on the door, shining his flashlight in my face. "Morning, ma'am. What brings you out here so early?"

"Delivery." His flashlight shines in back. "Important documents, y'know; archives no one got around to digitizing. They have to be there safe and sound by nine a.m. Guess who got the short straw? Should make it so long as there aren't any delays. Speaking of which, what happened here?"

"This? Ah, some idiots driving too fast most likely. Firing off weapons too, by the sound of it, and probably liquored up as well. You know how it is. Some people never learn. Well, you drive careful now. You don't want to end up like them."

"Surely don't. Have a better one."

He waves me on. As we reach the edge of the suburbs, two SUVs race by in the opposite direction. They're as black as night and bumper-to-bumper, just like in the movies. That puts a big, fat grin on my face. The Deep Web just drove straight by us and never saw a thing.

The first turn south will take us as far as it goes. That turns out to be not very far. The road dead-ends between isolated properties with a tangle of trees in front of us. We can't go back. Even now the locals must be telling the Deep Web about the lady they just let drive straight through. Yeah, you must have passed her on your way out here. They're gonna be pissed as hell.

Forward it is then, and south all the way. For that to happen, we need to know what's beyond these trees. First of all though, the muffled protests coming from behind me need to be taken care of. Boys, huh, they just can't sit still for five minutes. My daughter was so much quieter; but then, of course, she couldn't speak.

The boxes are dumped under a tree. We won't need them anymore. With the last couple still to go, Angie crawls out, brushing himself down as he says far too loudly, "Gee, thanks, Mom. Any longer and you might've damaged me permanently."

"Keep your voice down. You'll wake the neighbors. Now, come on. We're going for a walk."

Scrubland is what lies beyond, uneven and scattered with more trees. Not an easy walk by daylight; by starlight and half a moon, we can just about see our way. That's not a problem for me, but Angie decides he doesn't like it all, and, boy, does he start laying it on. "Hey, let's go for a walk. It's only the middle of the night and I can barely see a damn thing, but never mind, right? I just hope there aren't any scary monsters out here because I wouldn't want to accidently step on one and lose a leg."

"You'll lose more than a leg if you don't zip it. We're not out of this yet, and you're still making too much noise."

"Oh, I'm sorry. Oops! Look, I just walked into another tree. What dumbass put that there, I wonder."

"My God, will you quit with the whining? This isn't New York, y'know. Stuff just grows places."

"And then some lamebrain decides to walk through it in the middle of the night because the boogeyman's after her."

Dear, sweet Angie; the love of my life except when he's being a total pain in the ass. "They drove right by us on the road. That's how close they are, okay?"

"Yeah." He leans in toward me. "Well, sad to say, I didn't get to see your imaginary oppressors because of all of someone else's garbage you dumped on top of me."

We stand eyeball to eyeball, or at least we try to in the darkness. "Just . . . shut up and walk, okay? We need to be moving before they call in air support. Think you'll be able to see that, do you?"

"I dunno. I guess it'll depend on how much more garbage you decide to dump on me."

Frostily silent, at last we come to a riverbank. The only crossing in either direction is a railroad bridge. It'll have to do. Otherwise, we're looking at a major detour with checkpoints on all the roads in every direction. Also, the sky is lightening in the east. We need to be over that bridge before anyone for a mile or more can see us.

Back at the car, with Angie laboring every step of the way, we head back to the last intersection. A right turn brings us to a railroad crossing. The headlights die and we leave the pavement until a horrendous crunching grinds the car to a halt. Well, great. It never occurred to me it might not be able to handle off-road. It looked so good in the shop too.

If that wasn't bad enough, Angie decides this would be a good time to be helpful.

"Is that a train I hear coming?"

"No, but you're seriously asking for a slap."

He's grinning. It might be lost in shadow, but he's definitely grinning. Laugh it up, kid. While you're having fun, Mommy will figure it all out, starting with nursing the car back off the tracks. A few yards behind us is a property with a truck parked out front. It's well-worn, an old reliable, never given a day's trouble in all its years and easy to break into. With only the shortest of delays we're on our way again, bumping slowly toward the bridge. There's no turning back now. If a train comes in the next few minutes, we won't be seeing Mexico in this lifetime.

On the other side, there's a road running alongside the tracks. With the sun just peeping above the horizon, we pick up some speed. Tuttle is the first town we come to, its still-sleeping suburbs the perfect hunting ground for another vehicle someone's left out for the night. We soon find one and switch out our plates. Then we're gone like the night.

Mid morning, we arrive in Anson. We haven't slept or eaten since arriving in Oklahoma City so by now we're both tired and hungry. After a brief stop for takeout, we head out into the big country to find somewhere to eat and rest up. A derelict building along a dirt track to the west of town should serve well enough. Maybe it was a barn or a storehouse. Now it's all missing timbers and sun-bleached. It still has enough of a roof to give us shade from the sun and enough walls to hide us from passing eyes.

Side by side, we sit with our backs against the truck. At first, we eat in silence, just gazing out across the endless flat expanse of Texas, the light-brown earth of worked fields and the remaining stands of scrub. It's one of those moments that could almost be paradise, just me and him and no one else in the whole, wide world to bother us, until we hear the *chop-chop-chop* of a passing helicopter.

In between bites, Angie says, "Air support, huh?"

"Could be. Doesn't matter. They can't see us in here, and what are they looking for, anyway? A car some cop saw for a couple of minutes in darkness; and we've already dumped it, anyway."

"And all of that hours ago. The owner of this truck will have noticed by now, don't you think? Maybe the owner of those plates too. Seems to me we need some new wheels."

"Wow. You're learning fast. Keep this up and I might even make a professional out of you."

"I don't think so."

He's right, of course. The very idea is just the next level of corruption. It was innocence that drew me to him; my desire to possess something so utterly outside my own experience. Having possessed him, the very innocence that made him irresistible in the first place has been assaulted in almost every way, even to the point of dressing him up as a girl. There is very little left that could be done, short of actually making him shoot someone. Kansas City, Harrisburg, the broken-down woman outside St. Louis; it doesn't matter that none of that was meant to happen. It was me who put him there, and all of it in the service of my own ends. And yet, for all of that, here he still is, calling me to account. Well, okay. Now it's my turn, at least as far as it's safe to tell.

"You want my quid pro quo, babe? Because you were right, there are things I haven't told you. I kill people for a living. It's what I do. I don't even know how many people I've killed. I only know I'm good at it. I was one of the best, if not the best—until I met you. That's not an accusation. You haven't done anything wrong. It's all down to me. I didn't feel any guilt about it either. Why should I? They were rich. They were powerful. They were the kind who thought they were untouchable. If somebody wanted them dead, they probably deserved it. It was well paid too, my ticket into a lifestyle I couldn't even have hoped for otherwise, so why shouldn't I use it? I wasn't some street thug who was cheaper than a divorce lawyer. I was very precise, very controlled, and very expensive. Most of the time, the authorities didn't even know it was a takedown, and when they did . . . well, that's another cold case. Just throw it on the pile.

"Then I met you, or you walked into me, and it wasn't just my grocery bag you broke. You broke my world. You made me do things I would never have dreamed of before, and all of it while I still thought I was in control. I thought I was manipulating you, but all the time, you were manipulating me. That's the truth, isn't it? Just like I said when I came back from the High Line stabbed in the leg."

He laughs. "Wow. I mean, my God, can you hear yourself? Is there anything you can say that doesn't turn it all back on everyone else? You think I was manipulating you? I did what you wanted me to do. Having a gun waved drunkenly in your face'll do that to a person. After that I just went along with it—until you started killing people. Well, at least you've told one truth. It was all down to you. You didn't have to shoot that woman outside St. Louis. You chose to do that. And the pity of it is, you were doing so well up until then."

"I was doing so well up until then? What is that supposed to mean?"

"Hey, dumb ain't stupid, remember? Yeah, I walked into you on the street. Maybe that wasn't such an accident. Maybe I thought you'd be worth a couple of bucks, and you were. Maybe I thought you'd be worth a few more later. Course, I didn't know you were a cold, calculating bitch then. I know a whole lot more now. One of the things I still don't get though is why this road trip. Some guy stabbed you on the High Line and you shot him dead? Nah! You're too good to let something like that bother you. So, Mommy contract killer, what did you get messed up in? Who did you kill that every cop between here and Hell is supposedly after you?"

Whatever my silence might sound like to him, the truth is it's how a street kid becomes a prosecutor in just four days that's got me stumped.

"What? Puppies grow up too, y'know. A dog is for life, even when it's chewing up on your safe space. So who did you kill?"

Well, there's no going back now. "Some guy in DC. He worked for the government. I think he must have been involved in some kind of conspiracy or collusion because the guy I killed before him was some Russian mobster."

"Yeah, now we're getting to it. So not only did you piss off our government, you probably pissed off theirs as well. No wonder you're scurrying from corner to corner like a mouse in a nest full of rattlesnakes."

There's nothing like getting straight to it, and he's certainly doing that. Perhaps that's a good thing because it opens up a whole new world of problematic. There's an entire planet out there and none of it might be safe. We might end up inmates in a prison of our own making, the super villain and her henchboy just waiting for their super spy to turn up and end it all. Joey would've liked that. Joey would've reveled in it. Me, I'm putting it on the back burner. We gotta get out of this country first.

"We'll be fine. They haven't caught us yet, and I have more than enough money waiting for us so that they never will."

"Blood money. Money you made from killing people."

"Money I earned. Money I sometimes took considerable risks for. This ain't the movies, kid. You don't just walk into a room and beat up on five two-hundred-pound guys. I worked for that money. I planned, prepared, and prosecuted for it. Now you want me to just give it all away?"

"It's up to you. I'm not telling you what to do. I'm just saying, if you really are sorry, the path to redemption lies through sacrifice."

"Really? You're gonna start giving me religion like they haven't been killing each other for centuries? Yeah, guys, we're good with that. Just make sure it's not our people you're slaughtering. Well, I'm sure I'll give that the consideration it deserves."

And I do. There: it's done.

CHAPTER FOURTEEN

W e sleep where we sit, still resting against the truck and each other, until mid-afternoon. Almost immediately, his words return to hang around like a pervert in a washroom. What he means to achieve by planting that thought in my head is beyond me. It's almost like he's trying to save me or something, what with me being such a poor sinner and all. First of all, he demands no more killing. Now he demands all my hard-earned money is given away because he, or some other Being, doesn't approve. All that money that's waiting for us was made by my effort and my risk. It's about as deserved as it comes, and if there's some Higher Power out there that doesn't like it, tough.

As for my dear, sweet Angie, I'll just have to think of something to take his mind off it, or at least convince him he got what he wanted, because one thing's for sure. If we succeed in crossing the border, which we will, we're not going to end up subsisting in some favela in Rio. He, of all people, should know there's nothing remotely romantic or uplifting about that.

Angie drives, taking us back out onto the highway where we head west. Route 180 runs more or less straight in front of us: dirt-brown and pancake-flat on either side with only the occasional ranch or dwelling.

We make good time to somewhere, although it's doubtful either of us knows where that somewhere is. We could have gone on that way for hours, just cruising through this endless landscape, half-asleep to the world and beyond all care. Well, maybe not Angie. Wide awake, he nudges me out of my daydream and nods toward the mirror. Behind us is a cruiser, a state trooper by the looks of it. For what seems like forever, he hangs there. Maybe he's hoping for a reaction. That would be really stupid. This truck may be an old reliable, but it would be way out of its league in that contest.

My hand reaches for Angie's thigh. Not that he needs it. He's calm enough to just keep going, to wait it out until the trooper passes us by and speeds on ahead. That sets my alarm bells ringing. If he was checking us out, our stolen plates must have been reported by now, but he didn't pull us over. Angie is right. We need some new wheels. Before that, though, we need to get off this road.

We turn off Route 180 and head south on Route 126 until we reach Merkel. Next to I-20, we find a couple of places to eat. Choosing the one with outdoor seating because it's cooler than sitting in the truck, for a while, we eat in silence. Angie's guzzling noisily on his slushy but I ignore that, my thoughts turning to what we do next. Abilene seems like the answer. There should be good hunting there. Or we could try our luck . . .

A big, black SUV glides by. It has the word POLICE plastered all down its side, with a nice, big flash running through it, just to look cool and all. Maybe it's routine, or maybe the SUV slows just a little as it passes our vehicle by. That's the second time a cop's probably made our registration and then just driven off. Something is going on here, and Angie sees it too. "We got a problem?"

"No. Don't worry about it."

My super-blasé dismissal fails to convince him. "Don't worry about it? You're pretty laid-back all of a sudden for someone who thinks half the planet is after us."

"Don't worry about it. They got orders. They aren't going to do anything."

"Orders? What orders?"

"Be on the lookout for, report, don't approach, don't attempt to apprehend." He still doesn't get it. "They're tracking us. Somewhere out there, they're laying a trap. The only reason they haven't sprung one yet is they couldn't find us—and they won't be able to find us again once we've dumped the truck. So, come on. Drink up. We're taking the back roads into Abilene. We'll be safe enough there. The one thing they won't want when they make their move is witnesses."

"You seem pretty sure about that too."

"Have I been wrong yet?"

"Er, yes. Or have you forgotten that body we hid in the woods?"

Well, touché. "Just drink your slushy. The longer we sit here, the more time they have to prepare."

With lunch over, we drive back north out of Merkel, turning east on the first road we come to. North again and we come to a hamlet, turning east again on 605. Everything's going fine until Angie says, "We gotta stop."

"Why?"

"Because I gotta take a leak."

"You gotta what? Why couldn't you go in Merkel?"

"I didn't need to go in Merkel. I need to go now. So, can we stop?"

"My God, you just had to have that slushy, didn't you? Okay. Okay. We'll stop."

We come to a fenced-off plot with a hut in front and a square of four storage tanks behind. The gates are open with no sign of life. Once we're parked up, Angie disappears round the back, leaving me to pace back and forth because, damn kid, couldn't go before we left, could you.

A truck passes by. It slows to a halt, then backs up to block the entrance. My pacing stops because no one does that in the middle of nowhere. The driver steps out. In his battered Stetson, his worn jacket and jeans, and with those craggy features, he could pass for a rancher, but then, he could be almost anything. Thanks to Angie, the body in the woods is fresh in my mind. There'll be no going off half-cocked this time around.

He takes a couple of steps forward. "Afternoon, ma'am. Can I ask what you're doin' here?"

"Why?" My hands slide into the pockets of my windbreaker. The AR-15 is in the truck but the detective's firearm slips easily into my grasp. "Who wants to know?"

He stands with his right hand on his waist, his elbow slightly moving as his fingers work at his side. It could be entirely innocent. Maybe he's massaging an aching muscle. Or maybe he's got a weapon tucked into the back of his belt, just like that woman didn't, and he's setting up for a quick draw. It's impossible to be sure, but my hand tightens on the grip.

"Oh, I was just passin', is all. Folks don't usually stop hereabouts unless they got car trouble."

"I'm fine. Just wanted to stretch my legs. Thanks for stopping though. This is a long way from anywhere to be having car trouble."

"It surely is." He nods slowly, rubbing at his chin with his left hand. The rules haven't changed. Most of an assassin's job is still getting close enough without being made. So far, this guy is doing a pretty good job of it, but still, my firearm slips out to hide in the fold of my windbreaker. Either he leaves now or he's waiting for something.

"All done."

Oh my God. "Angie, get down!"

Assassin draws. We both duck and fire. A second shot has me scrambling for the cover of our truck, but Angie hasn't caught on yet. A third shot and he goes down. "Angie? Angie!"

Hunkered down behind our truck, my time is running out. Assassin is on the prowl, lining up a shot, but for the next few moments, the sight of Angie holds me rooted. He's lying there in the dirt with his arms spread on either side. It's impossible to know if he's alive or dead. Come on. Move. This is no time to be falling apart. Whatever state he's in, this business has to be dealt with first.

From our truck to the hut, there's only time enough for me to see blood running down the side of his face. That sends me cold inside. If he's dead, any promises that were made died with him. Deep Web or Network, that son of a bitch is gonna die.

Beyond the hut are the tanks, thick, squat, and rusting, and breathless silence. Assassin isn't coming straight at me. He must be behind one of the other three, with both of us listening and waiting. So it's cat-and-mouse then, with a tasty snack for the winner. His probably has a large number of zeros after it. Mine is vengeance, bittersweet. Only one of us is going to collect so let's get this show on the road.

Creeping out into the square, the firearm is leveled in front of me. A movement catches my eye beyond one of the tanks opposite. Damn! My shot is wasted on a shadow. Around the tank to my right and across to that tank, assassin has moved too. One misstep, mine or his, one well-placed shot, that's all either of us needs. Toward the fourth tank, and a bullet sings by me. My reply misses too. For a pair of professional killers, we both seem to be having something of an offday. A couple of deep breaths help to settle me. Come on, girl. You're better than him.

Once more into the square, step by step, slow and careful. Assassin darts across the gap between the two tanks opposite. We both fire and miss. He's not getting any closer, or maybe he's trying to run me out of ammo. Hats off for sneakiness, smart-ass, but it ain't gonna work.

Behind another tank, a few more breaths and it's all figured out. You think you're gonna sucker me. Let's see how much of a sucker you are. Slowly and carefully into the square again, one of us is playing by new rules. The other one isn't. He darts between two tanks, missing again. Been there, seen it, bought the T-shirt. It's Assassin School 101, fool. Never be predictable. Otherwise, someone like me might end up tracking you on a parallel course and then, suddenly, we come face-to-face. Firing first, my mag empties and he stumbles back, going down on his knees. He's wounded twice, shoulder and chest, but he's not done yet. He's raising his weapon. Not today, loser. Today you're on your back with my foot on your gun hand.

He looks up at me and smiles. "They said you were good."

"Well, at least they got that right." His weapon, a .45, is now mine. "So what's the deal with you, huh? I don't think I've ever seen such a piss-poor excuse for an assassin before. Did they actually think you were gonna take me down? I'm almost insulted, really. Oh, and just so you know" —The detective's firearm clicks at him a couple of times— "this one's empty. How about yours?"

In my sights, with his own weapon, this time, he laughs. "You weren't exactly shootin' so straight yourself, sweetheart, but then they also said you were a cunning bitch. Guess I should have paid closer attention."

"Who said? The Network?"

"Who else? After you killed that guy in DC, they came after all of us. So the directors cut a deal. We used to be independent. Now we're contracted to the state."

"And how is that my fault?"

"Yeah. Could've been any of us, right? Just wrong place, wrong time. No one cares, sweetheart. You're the sacrifice that saves the rest of us. They ain't gonna let you go. Accordin' to them, you already slipped through their fingers three times. Accordin' to what I was told, you slipped through ours twice as well."

"Twice? How so? There's only been those guys in Kansas . . ." At last, it dawns on me. "The High Line. That guy on the High Line was Network?"

"You betcha. They already decided to ditch you before everything went to shit."

"Why?"

"Dunno. The directors don't exactly discuss policy with us grunts. Maybe they just decided you were too hot. Or maybe they thought it was time you retired. You're not getting any younger, after all. There are sleeker, shinier models sittin' on the showroom floor, all just waitin' to be taken for a ride. Either way, you're punched out, sweetheart. You're off the books. They're gonna hunt you to the ends of the Earth, and we're gonna help them. But you run. You get as far away as you can. It won't make any difference because there'll always be another one of me waitin' around the corner, comin' through your front door or standin' at the bottom of your bed at two in the mornin'.'"

"You think? Well, they misled you, my friend. I'm a lot more than just good. I'll see them coming like I saw you. And then, when I'm good and ready, maybe I'll go after the directors. Maybe you could tell them that. Then again, maybe not."

A bullet through the head is hardly enough. Vengeance is a drug. So is fear, and the directors ought to be hooked on it like the little skank bitches they are. Maybe another time, with another messenger, since this one is no longer up to the task. Never mind. This little taste of instant gratification will have to do for now.

Such as it is, that satisfaction disappears on my return to Angie. He still hasn't moved. Please, God, don't let him be dead. Let there be a pulse. There has to be a pulse. At last, there is. He's alive; unconscious, but alive. The wound on the side of his temple is bad but the bullet appears to have bounced off. A glancing contact, but still . . . his skull must be as hard as a nut. A cut like that probably needs stitches, but a hospital is not an option. Neither is sitting around here thinking about it. In this landscape, who knows how many people heard that gunfire.

Thanks to assassin, we have a new vehicle. Unlike old reliable, this one is big, bullish, and almost new. We also have a small arsenal: another handgun, a pump-action shotgun, and a hunting rifle with scope. There's a first aid kit too, and a police scanner.

I drive the truck in next to Angie, hauling him to his feet and into the passenger's side. This eats up a couple of precious minutes. A few more are spent going back to search assassin, scoring a couple hundred bucks, several credit cards, IDs, and a black-bladed knife—military-grade by the looks of it. There's also the AR-15 in our old truck. What we need now is somewhere to go, somewhere we can lay low long enough for Angie to be patched up.

***

We're heading east along 605 again, with nothing but dust in our mirrors. The police scanner is crackling, but they're stumbling around in the dark. Assassin didn't drop a dime on us.

Angie starts to groan. My laugh is a spasm of relief. At least he's not in a coma. What other damage there might be is another question. "Baby? Can you hear me? Talk to me. Just say something. Tell me how you feel."

"Oh, my head. What happened?"

"You got shot."

"I got shot?"

Groggy and disoriented, he barely seems to understand.

"Yes, but don't worry about it, okay? I'm gonna take care of it. We just need to put some miles behind us first. So you sit back and rest up, all right?"

That's all the persuasion he needs, falling back into a drowse even as we come to a junction. Route 707 takes us south, a straight road into Tye and a large gas station and truck stop just north of I-20. By now it's early evening, but the place is still busy enough. Never mind. Concerned only for Angie, I park as far as possible from prying eyes. The first aid kit has pretty much everything, including glue, but we don't have any water. There's little point in trying to clean him up without it so, for now, covering up with surgical gauze will have to do.

"Angie. Angie babe, can you hear me? Keep pressure on this, okay? I'm going to leave you now, but not for long. Don't get out. Don't wander off."

Still barely with me, after some prompting at last he holds the gauze in place. As for the rest, so long as he's out of it, he's not going anywhere. Here's hoping he stays that way, at least for the next few minutes.

The convenience store is moderately busy. Just another traveler from somewhere to somewhere else, no one notices me. Still, there's no time to waste on browsing. I grab water and cleaning cloths, some snacks too because there ain't gonna be any eating out tonight, and, almost as an afterthought, some pain killers.

Back to the truck and the passenger-side door is open. Christ, no. No, no, no.

"Angie. Angie!"

He is nowhere to be seen and my thoughts begin to spiral into panic. The doors should have been locked. He should never have been left alone. We should never have come to this place. We should have made straight for Canada. We would have been safe by now. None of this would ever have happened. My God, he could be walking out into traffic right now.

No. Stop. Get a grip. If something had happened, everyone would know about it. Leave the purchases in the truck and go find him before someone calls the cops.

Out front, by the pumps, he's already attracted the attention of some guy and a couple of women. They're elderly and filled with concern, but also fussing indecisively as they look at his wound. Damn! Good Samaritans are the last thing we need, even if they probably did stop him from wandering off into the middle of the road.

Hurrying over, my relief comes out as a broad smile. "Oh, thank God. You've found him."

They look at me, sort of Gramma and Grampa disapproving. Yeah, yeah, bad Mommy went and messed up again.

"Is he with you?" says one of the ladies. "Only he was wandering around like he didn't know where he was."

"Yes. I'm sorry. I only left him for a moment. You know how it is."

They don't, which they make very clear with the glances they exchange. This needs to be wound up quickly, but now old guy says, "So how did he get that gash on the side of his head?"

With a ready explanation on the tip of my tongue, suddenly Angie decides to chip in with, "Someone shot me."

"Oh my Lord!" says one of the ladies.

"Why you poor thing!" says the other.

"Son," says old guy, "We need to get you to the hospital."

"No, really. That won't be necessary at all. He's just confused. The truth of it is we stopped a ways back to stretch our legs. Next thing I know, he's tripped on something and hit his head on a rock. It's no big deal. I was just about to clean him up."

"Well . . . maybe," says old guy. "It still looks pretty bad to me. Might even need stitches."

"No, it's fine. Really, he just needs some time to get over it. Thanks for finding him, but we really ought to get back to the car. The sooner he's resting, the better. Come on, baby. Let's leave these nice people to get on with their day."

Hurrying him away is no easy matter, and the Good Samaritans don't look at all like they bought my story. They watch us every step of the way, still fussing amongst themselves. It's pretty clear they're going to worry about it and worry about it until one of them just can't help but call the cops. Great! Now we're going to have to get the hell out of here as well.

Route 707 takes us south again until we come up to a lot on the edge of Tye. It's not gated, there's no one around, and there are some semi-trailers parked together in the middle of it. I pull up close in behind them so we're well hidden from the road. With the shadows lengthening, we should be safe for the night. Now, before the light goes, there's Angie to be dealt with.

"Come on, babe. Take these and then I'll clean you up."

The two painkillers in my hand he stares at like they're a salad or something. It's not an encouraging sign. He has to start getting over this soon because dragging an invalid around with me simply isn't going to work. God, that sounds so cold, but no amount of hating myself for even thinking it is going to change reality. This is a bad situation. If it comes to it, he won't just be dumped. He'll be found somewhere he can be safe until all of this is over.

"Please, Angie. Just take them. Everything will be fine, I promise."

At last, he does. Then he slumps back, barely conscious again. He might be concussed, but there's nothing to be done about that. All that can be done is clean the wound and glue it up; thankful he can't feel my blundering about. A real doctor would probably be horrified but, as far as this amateur can tell, it holds together well enough. For the next hour or so, as night falls, his breathing remains steady. He seems comfortable. He seems to be sleeping. That's the best thing for him.

CHAPTER FIFTEEN

A bright, sunny morning finds me yawning until once more panic seizes hold of me. The passenger-side door is open. He's wandered off again—but no, there he is, out front, taking a leak. Relief hardly covers it as, sitting back, my eyes close for an instant. Not only has he not wandered off but he seems to be back to himself again. In fact, seeing me watching him, he gives me a cheery smile and a wave. There was a bandage, but he isn't wearing it. He shouldn't have taken that off, but if he doesn't want it, it's hardly worth causing a scene. His wound still looks nasty, but it's holding together.

He walks back around the front of the truck with a certain swagger and jumps in beside me. "Hey, babe, I'm hungry. Let's get something to eat."

Me too, but we're not going back into Tye. With the sun well up, we leave it and any danger the Good Samaritans might have made a report behind. Running south through small town after small town, none of them have anything very much to offer. Angie is becoming increasingly restless;

fidgeting, drumming on the dash, and bursting out with comments like, "Wow, this place sucks," and, "Man, haven't they ever heard of a diner around here?"

"If you're that hungry, eat some of these snacks."

He's not interested. He wants real food. He wants action and bright lights, all the sparkly things, and now the specter of brain damage is starting to concern me. Please don't let it be that. Please let it be just a mild concussion. We can't go to a hospital, not until we're across the border. So please let it be something passing, for me as well as for him.

Still early enough to call it breakfast, we reach San Angelo. After a little cruising, we find a burger place and Angie is close to ecstatic. "Yeah, now this is what I'm talking about! Come on. Let's eat!"

He's out and heading for the entrance before the truck has a chance to stop, leaving me feeling a mite irritated. "Well, okay then. Thanks for waiting, sweetheart."

My mood isn't improved when I follow him inside. The restaurant is slightly over half full, which is fine. The problem is he's draped himself halfway across the counter and he's talking to a server with a big, silly, eager grin on his face. Newly out of high school by the looks of her, she's all blonde curls and peaches and cream, and he's trying to hit on her, badly. "So, whaddya say? You wanna bunk off while the boss ain't looking? Maybe we could go round the back and make out for a while."

With barely concealed contempt, she glares back at him. "You want extra fries with that . . . sir?"

"Aw, come on. It'll be just you, me, and the dumpster. You—"

"Hi. Can you make whatever he ordered for two? That would be great."

For me, she manages a smile. Angie she leaves with another dagger stare, with me adding, just in case he missed it, "And you'd better start behaving yourself. The last thing we need is to be attracting attention to ourselves."

"Oh, lighten up! I was just trying to be friendly."

"Well, try being a little less friendly, at least until you've learned how. Okay?"

"Okay, *Mom*. Whatever you say, *Mom*. I'll be a good boy from now on, *Mom*."

The girl returns with our order.

"Take these, sweetie. Find a booth. I'll be with you in a minute."

"Yeah, *Mom*." He takes the bags and starts to walk away. "Can I start without you, *Mom*?"

The two of us watch as he heads for a booth by a window. This display, that there is a nastier side to whatever's going on with him, has only increased my concern. Maybe that bullet did enough damage to mess him up completely, like a whole new personality. No, that doesn't even bear thinking about. It's just a mood swing, that's all. He just needs something to calm him down.

"You wouldn't happen to have something, would you? You know, just to chill him out. It's no big deal. It's just that he gets a little over-excited sometimes."

"I guess that bang on the side of his head isn't helping either, huh."

"Yeah, that too. It was an accident. He just needs a little time to get over it."

She thinks about it. That's okay. A side of downers is probably not something she gets asked for everyday. While she takes her time, my motherly concern oozes like melted cheese until, at last, she decides she's good with it. "Just give me a minute, okay? I'm sure I can find something."

Over at our booth, Angie's already started. Again, thanks for waiting, sweetie.

"Is it good?"

"Yeah, *Mom*. It's, like, yummy."

"Okay. You can quit with the attitude now. You've made your point."

"Really? Oh, wow. I'm so pleased."

"Yeah, really. Quit it. Now! Just because we're in Texas doesn't mean you can start acting like you just came in from a month herding cattle on the range."

"Aww, shucks. I was only havin' some fun. I ain't even shot nobody yet—unlike you."

He holds my gaze, just spoiling for a fight. This we don't need, not in the middle of a busy restaurant, but if that's how it's gonna be . . . Before either of us can start bumping heads though, the girl walks by, leaving two tablets on the table in passing. Angie looks at them, with all that attitude crystallizing into a deep suspicion. "And what are those for?"

"I'm worried about you. You got shot in the head yesterday. These are just to chill you out a little, until this mood you're in passes."

They're in my hand, like a peace offering, but he's not buying it. "Really."

"Yes. Please, baby, I'm doing this for you. You're not right. You're all jumpy and in everyone's face. That's not who you are."

"Uh-huh. So what you're saying is, I'm not docile enough for you. You want me all nice and quiet and sweet, like I was when I was wearing a dress."

"No! Of course not. I was wrong to do that to you. I just—"

He strikes out at my hand, sending the tablets flying. "Manipulation! That's all it is with you. You can't talk to anyone without figuring out how to use them, how to control them. And now you want to control me . . . with drugs. Well, screw you, bitch! I'm not gonna be your toy any longer."

Scattering food across the table as he stands, probably deliberately, he stalks out hunched with rage. The entire restaurant is watching until they see me watching them. Yeah, so! Think whatever the hell you like. All that matters to me is how to calm him down. The person who manipulated and abused him isn't here anymore. He has to understand that.

Outside, he's standing by the truck with his head in his hands. His low, almost animal moans are as painful as a dull blade. At least no one else is around to hear them.

"Oh, baby. Baby, what's the matter?"

"My head. It feels like it's exploding."

"I know. Really I do. Now come on, get in the truck. You need rest, not all of this excitement."

He doesn't resist my guiding hand, but the tension within him seeps through it into me. If only it would all seep through, bringing his pain with it. Make it mine, just as the fault is mine. Let me carry this burden so that he might be free again. As much as this is making me want to cry for him though, these are all just empty wishes. All that can be done this side of the border is to settle him into the passenger's side, climb in beside him, and offer him painkillers. "Take these. They'll help, I promise."

There are no accusations this time, no suspicion or outrage. Meekly, he takes them, slumping back with beads of sweat glistening on his forehead. It's almost unbearable to watch, as unbearable as thinking this might be permanent. He must start showing signs of recovery soon. He must come back to me. His old self must still be in there; the tenderness, the caring, the abhorrence of violence, and everything else that made him my conscience. It's just hiding away from the pain, that's all. So fight it, baby, or at the very least hang on. The help you need is coming. As God is my witness, the help you need is coming.

★★★

South again, and late morning brings us to Sonora. Angie has slept all the way. That suits me fine. So long as he stays that way we should be able to come and go as quietly as a passing breeze.

Just to be sure, we drive on by the gas station and truck stop just north of I-10. Too much risk of another incident like Tye there. As the tank fills at a local gas station, my thoughts turn to what we ought to do next. A little shopping wouldn't be a bad idea. We could certainly do with a change of clothes. Add to that a shower, since both of us must stink by now. Deodorant will have to do. It won't be for long. The border is only a few hours away. We could be in Mexico by dusk. We could—

Another truck pulls up behind us. It's light gray with a white star on its door. It's the sheriff, showing up at just the wrong moment, like they do. He gets out, broad-shouldered and just a touch paunchy but with an open, friendly face and a broad smile. "Morning, ma'am."

"Morning. Sorry. I'll be out of your way in a minute."

"Oh, there's no hurry. One thing we got plenty of around here is time."

"Small town, huh?"

He walks forward, checking out our plates and our tires along the way. "That's right. We haven't had any real desperadoes round here since Sheriff Briant shot Bill Carver dead in the store. He rode with Butch Cassidy's Wild Bunch, y'know."

"Wow. That's some local history, right there."

"Oh, we got more than that." He's pleased as punch for the opportunity to talk up the town. "We got caves and a nature preserve and a museum too, if you're so inclined. Is that your boy asleep in the truck there?"

"Yeah. We've been on the road awhile. You know how quickly they get bored. Well, I think I'm about done. I'll just move out of your way."

"Now don't you worry about that. You just head on in and pay. We'll still be here when you get back."

"Why, thank you. I'll be real quick, I promise."

One more look at Angie before making my way in to pay shows me he's still asleep. We should be fine, but barely a minute of browsing later, a gunshot shatters the peace. Everyone looks in its direction, with someone at the counter saying, "Oh my Lord. That boy just shot the sheriff!"

Oh my Lord, indeed. This is Texas. Everyone owns a gun. Outside, the sheriff is lying on his back with his hands raised to either side. Standing over him with a gun pointed at his head is Angie, and he's screaming, "Where is she? Where is she?"

Oh, crap! "Angie? My God, Angie, what are you doing?"

He glances at me. "Son of a bitch was hanging around, snooping and asking questions. I thought maybe he took you away, like, I'd have to rescue you again."

"No. I was just inside paying for gas. Now, put the gun away, baby. You don't have to be doing this."

"Put the gun away? Are you insane? He's the sheriff, for chrissakes!"

"Angie. Listen—"

"No, you listen. Take his gun. Do it! Take his gun."

He's a wild thing, high on adrenaline, and it'll be a noose around both our necks if he pulls that trigger. The only way to control him right now is do what he wants.

"Okay. Okay. I'm taking his gun."

The sheriff watches me hunker down next to him. His face is not quite so open and friendly now. At least he doesn't appear to be bleeding. Angie didn't shoot him after all, but that's about as sunny as it gets. Dark clouds are gathering in his eyes. They're the kind that say, "You best shoot me now because you're plain out of welcome." What he needs is some reassurance, a few kind words, but the only ones that come to me are, "I'm really sorry about this. He's just not been himself lately."

Not good. Bill Carver must have seen that look too, just before he ended up dead, but it's too late to say sorry. The spirit of Sheriff Briant is saddling up, and he don't take kindly to flippancy. Not that this sheriff is going to do anything while some crazy kid is holding a gun on him. "His keys. Take his keys as well."

Okay. We've come this far without anything bad happening. It's time for one more appeal, as unthreateningly as possible. "Angie. Please. Lower the gun. You don't—"

"Get in the truck!"

"Angie, please—"

"Get in the goddam truck, woman!"

Meekly compliant or just too stunned to believe he's talking to me like that, the truck is a slow walk beyond him. There's a gun in my hand. It would be easy enough to knock him unconscious. It would be easier still to shoot him. Don't even think it. This is not his fault. He's hurt. He needs help. That's my burden here, my need, the obligation that cannot be walked away from.

Halfway around the front of our truck and there are two more shots. Oh, Christ, no; but the sheriff is still unharmed. Angie has put two bullets through the grille of his truck. He turns, sees me standing there, and screams, "Get in the truck! No, the other side. I'm driving."

He runs for the driver's side. The engine roars and we tear out of the gas station as if every lawman in Texas is after us. They soon will be, not to mention the Deep Web and the Network. We haven't paid for our gas, either. Quite why that should be of concern to me is a mystery. It certainly won't be to them.

Angie speeds us westward out of town and onto the frontage road next to I-10. He's almost maniacal, still high on adrenaline and careening the truck down the center of the road like we're running moonshine or something. This is genuinely scary, and it has to stop. "Angie, sweetheart. Slow down."

"Why?" He's grinning like a fool. If there was a posse behind us, he'd be shooting at it. "What are you afraid of? We're Monster Mom and Angel, remember? They can't touch us."

"Why? Because running is the fastest way to get caught. Angie, you have to listen to me. We need to get off this road. We need to dump this vehicle. We need to stop looking like we're running. Now please, slow down, stop."

He throws me a glance, then a second one. He's still grinning, but it's not quite so foolish anymore.

"Angie. Stop the truck. Let me take over. I know what I'm doing. You know that."

We begin to lose speed, the truck, at last, rolling to a halt in the middle of the road. His hands are still gripping the wheel, but that grin is fading fast, giving way to a look of horror. "I did that, didn't I? I nearly shot that guy."

"It's all right. You didn't hurt him. Well, maybe you dented his pride a little, but I'm sure he'll get over that eventually."

"But I could've, couldn't I? I could've been like that guy who killed my parents."

His mood is collapsing into remorse, which is almost as bad as his euphoria. This is becoming a roller-coaster ride, with me struggling to be anything more than a passenger. There could be an actual posse in our rearview at any moment, but we're not going anywhere until he's been picked up off the floor.

"You didn't know what you were doing, okay? You woke up; I wasn't there. Maybe you panicked. That's as much my fault as it is anybody's. Look, it'll be all right, but you gotta let me drive. You gotta let me get us out of here like I did in New York and all those other places. You know I can do this, so let me do it now. Come on, baby. Change places with me."

Slowly, dejectedly, he nods. That's one hurdle overcome. Now to figure out exactly what the hell we are going to do next. Just up ahead is a compound. As we approach, there's a sign on the chain-link fence that says it's a supply company. At the front of the lot is a single-story building. Behind is a yard. Parked just within sight of the highway is an SUV, the perfect vehicle for where we're going. As we pull up beside it, there is just Angie to deal with. "Let me take care of it, okay? No surprises."

Another nod, but just to be sure, the only gun we're carrying is in my hand. As we walk around the back of the SUV, some guy appears. He's jowly and paunchy, which has me guessing he mans the phones, handles the paperwork, and snacks a lot.

"Ma'am." He's all bright and breezy. "Can I help you, because—"

Until the gun is in his face. "You surely can. I'm here to pick up some supplies, like the keys to your vehicle and any money you've got. Now, let's step inside and do the paperwork. That okay with you?"

"Yes, ma'am." One hand goes up, the other reaches into a pocket for his keys.

"Take them and start moving our stuff." Angie hardly seems to hear me. He has become like an automaton waiting to be wound up. "Angie! Take the keys and move our stuff."

Trudging like it's the end of the world, at last he goes. He'll be fine. He better be, because there's this guy to deal with. We go inside and not a moment too soon either. As sirens go screaming by outside, he knows who they're for. "You ain't gonna shoot me, are you?"

"Not if you're good. Now find me some rope or something and then get face down on the floor."

A few minutes later, he's hogtied and gagged. Angie is already in the SUV, and so are all our guns. Back out on the frontage road, at the first opportunity, we cut across I-10 to head north along a back road into a landscape of scrub and nodding donkeys.

CHAPTER SIXTEEN

S parse cloud has turned to overcast. It matches our mood as, for the next hour or so, we wind our way northwest. The scrubland is unchanging, the service roads deserted. Angie sits beside me, head back and silent, as low as he's ever been. Talking to him, trying to offer him comfort and reassurance, makes no difference. He's hiding somewhere inside himself, a lost soul in silent turmoil.

There must be some way to snap him out of it, to bring him back to me; so at last, the SUV comes to a halt in the middle of nowhere. We should be safe enough. This close to the border, they'll be expecting us to head south. That's why we're making for New Mexico, where we should be out of reach of the Texas authorities at least.

For a while, we sit in silence beneath the threatening clouds. Watching him rest, it almost feels like a crime to disturb him, but my need to know outweighs that. Tell me what's going on in there, baby, so we can work it through together.

"Angie. Can you hear me?"

Feeling his hand gently squeezed, he opens his eyes, taking a moment to focus on me. His gaze seems far away, as if he doesn't want to see me. It feels like an accusation, a stab to the heart, but this is not about me or those glowing embers of guilt. This is about him. My hand rises to stroke his cheek and feel his brow. "How do you feel? Are you all right?"

He shifts a little, finding a more comfortable position. "I'm good. How are you?"

"I'm good too. How about you and me get out and stretch our legs while there's no one around to bother us?"

"No. I like it here."

"I know, but we've got a long way to go, and I want to make as few stops as possible."

He fixes on me with a sudden intensity, his mood change like quicksilver. "Why? You afraid if we stop I might try to shoot someone again? You think I'm out of control, don't you? You think I'm some kind of nutjob psycho, like you."

Hearing those words, my heart dies a little. He's still so far from me, and maybe gone forever, but so long as there's still breath in both of us, this nutjob psycho isn't giving up. "Angie, listen to me. You didn't shoot anyone, but you don't go around sticking a gun in a sheriff's face, either, least of all in Texas. That's why I don't want to stop. The sooner we're across the state line, the better. As for the rest, you're not that kind of person. Believe me, I know. I've met real psychos. You just need to take the time to find yourself again, that's all, because the real you is sweet and loving.

The real you would never intentionally hurt anyone."

"So you're not afraid of me?"

"Oh, sweetheart. Why would I be afraid of you? I love you. I will always love you."

His gaze is thoughtful and measured, as if he's weighing me and finding me wanting. It used to be open and innocent. Maybe there is nothing left here but straws to be clutched at. Maybe what's sitting here beside me has been changed forever. Not yet, it seems, for at last he smiles. "And I love you too, baby. Okay then, let's go stretch our legs."

We get out of the truck. Already spots of rain have started to fall. As they quickly turn into a shower, Angie holds out his hand. He laughs, and he's that person again, the one who's seen the worst this world can throw at him yet still rise above it. This is the person who has already begun to teach me how to do the same—like standing here in a rain shower in the middle of nowhere and finding nothing but joy in it. With his hand in mine and my laughter joining his, he pulls me around to face him, taking my other hand as well. "Beth. Do you realize I've never actually called you Beth before? That is your real name, isn't it? Because I'd hate to think it was just another lie."

"It's not a lie. My full name is Bethany Jo Leland, and I'm from Michigan."

"Well, hello, Bethany Jo Leland from Michigan. I'm from Connecticut and my name is Benjamin Franklin Hirst. Yeah, my parents were into that whole Revolutionary thing, y'know. I used to like the re-enactments; the uniforms, the parading around, the volleys of musket fire, until—"

"Oh, baby." There are rivulets of rain running down his cheeks like tears. Let them cleanse him of his pain. Let me help by gently brushing them away. "You see, this is who you are: a boy from Connecticut called Ben. Not some wild outlaw riding into town and trying to shoot the sheriff. You should know by now. That's *my* job."

"Yeah." He leans in so our foreheads touch. "Because my job is saving you, right? So how's the boy from Connecticut doing, huh?"

"Well enough, I suppose. Just leave the life-or-death stuff to me from now on, okay? And I promise I won't kill anyone unless I absolutely have to. Now, how are you going to show me how much you love me? I may be a contract killer and a total bitch, but I still have needs and desires. So come on, baby, show me how much you love me."

"Okay."

We kiss, our bodies meeting to share their warmth in the coolness of the rain. Hands move, exploring each other beneath wet clothing. Gently at first, but then with increasing urgency, we strip each other and sink naked to our knees. As one we begin to move together, with my heartfelt whisper going up to the gray and weeping sky. "Please, baby. Please come back to me."

***

The sky above is lighter, the clouds long since drained—as are we. Still naked, the chill of damp skin and moist earth makes me shiver. He, of course, has fallen asleep.

A gentle nudge rouses him. "Come on, babe. We'd better get moving."

We clean ourselves and our clothes as best we can. They're damp, but they will dry soon enough with wearing. Then it's north and west again, until a highway takes us into a small town. On the other side of railroad tracks is a bar. By now, it's late afternoon, and there are several vehicles outside. Their owners must all be inside. Parked in amongst them, we wait. No one comes out. No one arrives. It's never going to be safer than now for me to slip out and switch plates with one of them. With that, we're gone, without anyone ever knowing we were there.

Three and a half hours later, we cross into New Mexico, stopping off in Hobbs for something to eat. The restaurant is less than half full, but it's still busy enough. We hole up by a window and mind our own business. Angie seems quite relaxed; although there is something slightly off about the little smile he's wearing. It better not mean anything. All we need is one more day. The border is that close.

"You happy? You look happy."

"I'm as happy as this burger. But then, it's made from a dead cow."

Okay. Not quite what was hoped for, but if he wants to be playful . . . "Well, at least it's not causing any more climate change. Hey, that would make a good bumper sticker, don't you think? 'Stop climate change. Eat a cow.' That should confuse all those vegan eco-warriors. And don't forget the bison, water buffalo, and wildebeest as well. I mean, they fart too, right?"

He holds my gaze, not quite sure whether to take me seriously or not. You started this, kiddo. Come back at me with your best shot.

"Okay." He's thinking about it. "So, if we kill all the big animals because their farting causes global warming, what are we going to eat?"

"Well, I guess we'll all have to eat beans. You like beans, don't you?"

"Yeah, but beans make you fart too, don't they? Won't that just cause more global warming?"

"So what do you want to do then? Kill everything that farts? Bees fart too, y'know. If you kill all the bees, who's going to pollinate the plants?"

"Yeah, right!" He snorts loudly. "Bees fart. Now you're just making it up. Besides, killing everything is your thing, not mine."

"Nope. I'm a businesswoman, an entrepreneur. I spotted a gap in the market and exploited it. That's free-market capitalism, baby, and black market communism. If you've got the money to pay for it, someone will supply it. And I never did anything without someone paying me to do it. So, if you want to stop global warming, how am I any different than the guy who killed that cow, which, by the way, you're still eating? Oh yeah, and bees actually do fart.

So do termites—quite a lot, in fact. And there are a helluva lot more of them on the planet than there are cows."

With a shake of his head, he turns to look out the window. It's a silly conversation and he's done with it, or he doesn't have an answer so he's not playing anymore. Poor baby. As well as all the other things we're going to do, we're going to have to get you a proper education because that's no way to win an argument.

At the same time a group of kids arrives, high-schoolers not quite old enough yet to trick their way into a bar. They're boisterous. They sit at a table in the middle of the restaurant. Angie looks across at them. He shifts in his seat, stretching one leg along it while he rests his back against the wall. It's like he's decided they're trouble and he's going to keep an eye on them. My eye stays on him because who knows where this might be going. In fact, it's time we were leaving. "Come on, Angie, finish up. We've still got a long ways to go."

"Nah." He pushes his food away. "I'm done with that. And why are you still calling me Angie? You know my name."

"Yes, but Angie's the name I'm familiar with. Call it my special name for you, if you like. No one but you and me gets to use it."

"No one but you and me, huh? Wow. Is that because we're in love and all?"

"Well . . . aren't we?"

"Oh, I worship the very ground you walk upon. I live only for your approval. Can't you see how well you trained your puppy?"

"Okay, that's it. Come on . . . Ben. We're leaving."

Beating me to it, he stands loud and proud as he announces, "Hey, everyone. This is Bethany Jo from Michigan and we're in love. Ain't that just the greatest thing in the whole, wide world?"

Most of the customers just sit there with bemused looks on their faces. The high-school kids begin to snigger, especially the two girls as they whisper to each other behind their hands. One of the boys, with lank, shoulder-length hair and one of those in-your-face T-shirts, decides to do more, calling back at him, "Yeah, man, like, that's awesome. Maybe your mom shouldn't let you drink at dinner, y'know?"

The teenagers snigger some more. It's not their fault. They're not to know they're pouring water onto burning oil. Instantly bullish, with his shoulders tensed and his fists clenched, Angie takes a few steps toward them. "What's that supposed to mean, smart mouth? You calling my woman a pedo or something?"

The teenagers aren't sniggering anymore. All the other customers have stopped eating. The staff has stopped serving. All that's needed now is for one of them to call the local law.

"Baby. Come on. Leave—"

"No! You think I'm going to let that jackass talk to you like that? No one talks to you like that!"

A couple of older guys have risen to their feet. For now, they're just standing by. Meanwhile, lank hair has a look that's close to terror on his face. "No, man, I was just saying, like . . . I'm sorry. I didn't mean anything by it."

Angie turns on him again. "Oh yeah? You wanna know what I think? I think you need your mouth shut, like, permanently."

He moves. The two older guys move too, zeroing in to intercept him.

"Angie, stop! Stop this now!" Grabbing at his arm is useless. He isn't listening to me and he won't be stopped.

One of the older guys steps into his path. "Now just hold up a moment. There's no need for this. The kid was just making a bad joke is all."

Each of these guys on their own could make mincemeat out of him, but still, Angie glares up at this one like they're both heavyweights psyching each other out before a bout. "Is that right. And who are you to come sticking your face in?"

"I'm the guy who likes to eat in peace. So why don't you be peaceful before I shut *your* mouth."

They're eyeball to eyeball. It's plain the older guy doesn't want to do this, but if he has to, he will. The other guy stands to one side, hardly needed but just as ready. Everyone else is watching, waiting. There ought to be phones out by now, if not to call the cops, then certainly to video it because who needs the Coliseum when there's video sharing? Before anyone does think of it, there's one more chance to try to reason with Angie. "Come on, sweetheart, walk away. You heard what the man said. It was a bad joke. Just let it go."

He still isn't listening. Well, okay then. Better he's forced to it by me than them. "Angie, think. Look at these guys. You can't win, even if I wanted you to try, which I don't. Now come away because I'm not going to let you do this. You're not protecting me. You're just picking a fight."

His answer is a seething glare, its hostility as raw as it is impotent. Unable to put it into words, he turns and stalks out, leaving me to stand with eyes closed and feeling just as frustrated. We're so close to freedom but, with every step we take, he puts it more in jeopardy. Something has got to change.

There's only more trouble to be had with him out there alone, but even as my hand reaches for the door one of the older guys decides he's just gotta share. "That kid's not right in the head, lady! You need to get him seen to!"

Yeah. Tell me about it, genius.

Out in the parking lot, Angie is pacing like a caged animal. For a few moments, we are alone together but yards apart. Kindness, supportiveness, sympathy, trust—all of them have been tried and, every time, he just slips through my fingers again. Hell, even sex has failed. All the way until now my promise has stood unbroken, but this has got to stop. It's simply too dangerous.

"Angie!"

"What!" He comes straight at me. "You humiliated me, again. You've done nothing but humiliate me. From the first day you—"

My slap turns his anger instantly to shock. It's a betrayal that stings me too but, right now, there is nothing else. "Yes, I promised I would never hurt you again, but now you're hurting both of us. Can't you see that? You think you're protecting me? You're not. You're just making things harder. You think I'm being unfair? You think I don't know how I treated you? Well, how many apologies do you want? How many times are you going to keep picking at it? It's over, Angie, it's done, and so will we be if you don't start getting back in control of yourself. Or is that what you want? Do you want me to dump you by the side of the road again? Do you want me to just walk away? Hell, I'll even give you all our money if you want it. Well, is it? Is that what you want?"

He doesn't answer. He's still too stunned. That's a good thing because my frustration has brought me close to being burning oil too: fit to explode at the first drop of water. That drop comes as one of the guys from inside the restaurant shouts at me, "Jeez, lady. That's no way to treat a kid."

Really! He's across the parking lot. The other guy is standing just behind him, and the windows of the restaurant are filled with gawping faces. Look at them with their righteous disapproval, all thinking *how awful. What a terrible person she is.* Well, screw every damn one of you. There's already enough guilt here without you butting in.

As for loudmouth, they all watch me march toward him. Maybe it's my imagination, but he doesn't seem quite so sure of himself anymore. Good, because this mom's wrath is about to be delivered upon him. "Here's the thing, and please do correct me if I'm wrong, but, a couple of minutes ago, weren't you ready to beat the crap out of him?"

The poor lamb seems rather hurt by that. "I was trying to stop a fight. I wouldn't have actually—"

"Oh yeah!" He gets a slap too, harder even than Angie's. "You mean a fight like this? So come on, big guy. What are you gonna do? You gonna hit a woman?"

Of course not. He's not that kind. We both know it, but right now my fury is way beyond giving a damn. "I didn't think so. What happens between me and my son is none of your goddam business, got it? So why don't you take your big, fat, burger ass and waddle off somewhere else with it."

Instead, he decides to say out loud what all of them are thinking. "Lady. You're not fit to be a mother."

"Oh yeah! So go tell a judge!"

Since he might just do that, Angie is bundled into the SUV, and Hobbs becomes the next town we leave in a hurry. This is getting to be way too much of a habit.

CHAPTER SEVENTEEN

O nce again we're on service roads. If anyone at the
restaurant in Hobbs has reported us, it's unlikely the
local law will find us out here. We're both in a subdued
mood, as silent as the emptiness we're passing through. Two
hours later, we cross the Pecos, and the joke is just too good
to pass on. "Well, I guess God just quit on us."

Angie casts me a glance, his expression deadpan, like,
not funny. So it's the silent treatment again, and this time it
isn't semi-fake. Not until we come to a junction in Artesia
with a sign pointing to Roswell does he perk up. Then
the raging bull becomes a school kid, all fired up with
enthusiasm as he says, "Hey, look at that. Can we go?"

"Can we go where?" The answer is as plain as that sign,
but if this gets him talking.

"Roswell. I'd like to see a UFO. Wouldn't you?"

"And you believe all that stuff, do you?"

"Well, yeah. I knew a couple of guys in New York. Both
of them swore they'd been kidnapped by aliens. They even
had those implants under their skin. Man, they could tell

you some stories. Real scary stuff. Like, it completely ruined their lives."

"Yeah. I can think of a few other things that probably ruined their lives, but okay, if you wanna go, we'll go. Don't be surprised if all the little gray men turn out to made of plastic though."

"Have some faith, Mom. The Network won't find us if we're on another planet."

"Faith! You do know what aliens do to people, don't you? Well, obviously you do if you've met some of their so-called victims."

"Of course, but that's okay. If they don't play nice, you can just shoot them in the face."

"Right, because what could go wrong with that."

Hanging a right, an hour later, we cruise into town.

In the center is a museum, but this late in the day, it's closed. Angie is disappointed. Never mind. He doesn't want to see some made-up displays. He wants to see the real thing. We head west out of town and find somewhere quiet to park. Away from the highway, it should be safe enough. If anyone comes along and starts asking questions, we're just another pair of UFO hunters hoping to see something, even if it is only a secret test flight.

Side by side, we lie on our backs gazing up at the night sky. Against the backdrop of the Milky Way and a billion stars, a single pinprick glides by hundreds of miles above us.

"Look." Angie points up at it. "Is that one?"

It's almost a shame to disappoint him. "No. That's more than likely the space station. Just think, there actually is somebody up there looking down at us."

"Yeah. You got that right."

We fall silent. He might be hoping to see some light descend from the sky, but it's the immensity of it all that's got me thinking, the sheer enormity that dwarfs us and our little lives. Beneath our city lights, we are blind to our insignificance. We come, we go, and all of that never even notices. A million years from now, someone else will be walking this Earth. They will know nothing of us once all the steel has rusted and the books have turned to dust, the plastics eaten and the glass ground back to sand. All that will be left are a few landing sites on the moon, except of course that never happened. Yeah, there's many an hour been wasted watching those videos, and the flat earthers and the ghost hunters.

If Angie's life had turned out differently, he might be sitting in his mom's basement watching them right now. He isn't. He's here with me. The warmth of his hand is right there in mine, a small beacon in the coolness of the night and the vastness of the universe. It doesn't matter if there's anyone up there watching us or not. This is our little part of it all, just him and me together, and finally, it's time because my little tragedy hardly even begins to compare with all of that.

"Angie, are you awake?"

"Yeah."

"Good, because there's something else I need to tell you. First of all though, you gotta promise me you won't get mad."

"Get mad? Why would I get mad when I'm just lying here chillin' with the universe?"

"Because that's all you've been doing lately."

"Okay. I promise. So what's the big secret?"

"I told you I killed my parents."

"I know, but you never said why. Me and the universe, we're all ears, so I hope this is gonna be good."

Putting it like that isn't exactly helping, but then, given his mood swings, it's not really that much of a surprise. Squeezing his hand, partly to reassure myself but also hopefully to keep him from losing it, there's no other way to begin this than just say it. "My parents decided to have me circumcised."

"What? You mean like that thing they do to girls in Africa?"

"No. I mean like for real circumcised."

The universe continues to gaze silently down on us, no longer visible to me because my eyes are closed. If there is anybody out there, apart from those astronauts, please don't let him lose it.

He sits up, his hand slipping from mine. "For real circumcised. Like . . . you were born a boy?"

Well, the cat's out of the bag now. "Yes, but the doctor screwed up, cut it clean off. I don't know what happened exactly. Maybe he slipped. Maybe he was incompetent. Back then, the best all those other doctors could come up with was to tell my parents to raise me as a girl."

"But . . . they could have done, y'know, reconstructive surgery, couldn't they?"

"Dunno. No one ever talked about it; not to me anyway. I came from a small town in the rust belt; not much education and even less money, and my parents weren't exactly the brightest. I guess they must have gotten some kind of settlement. If they did, I don't know what they did with it. All I know is I ended up going to school in a dress. It didn't take me long to figure out something wasn't right, but that just led to counseling. They told me nice girls didn't beat up on their classmates. Nice girls didn't break things. Nice girls didn't get into trouble or end up being sent to juvie.

"I learned fast. I started playing nice. Then one day, me and my mom had a knock-down, drag-out fight and she just dumped it right out there in front of me. She tried to take it back, of course. She tried to give me all that 'I don't know why I said that' stuff, but it was too late. I hated her. I hated all of them. I wanted them to hurt too, but how? How could I make them hurt like they hurt me?

"I ended up with two options: suicide or revenge. I chose revenge. I blew my parents up in a gas explosion. I don't know where I got that idea from, but I used to sneak into movie theaters all the time. That was twenty years ago. The authorities never suspected me, of course. I was just the poor little girl who somehow got out with a teddy bear clutched between her baby breasts. Aww, poor thing. Now she's all alone in the world.

"They handed me over to child services and I ended up in a foster home. It was little more than a money factory for the people running it, and the ten of us who lived there knew it. So long as we were careful and the money kept coming in, we could do pretty much whatever we liked.

"I wasn't so careful. I got a reputation for being difficult. They threatened me with drugs, and worse, so I skipped with one of the boys. I told him I loved him. I didn't. I just wanted to get out of there. I think he had some fantasy in his head where we were going to be the new Bonnie and Clyde; that we'd eventually go down together in a hail of bullets. He was a real romantic like that—or just plain nuts. He did prove to be a useful idiot though, teaching me how to fire and clean a gun and introducing me to my first contacts.

"Then one day, the cops came storming through the door and blew his brains out. I curled up in a corner and pretended I was being held against my will, like a sex slave or something. It was easy enough, since they never bothered to check. I was a victim and that was good enough for them. I got a couple of nights in a hospital out of that, full room and board, until I skipped outta there too.

"Pretty soon after that, I had a career, though at first I had to fight for it because the underworld has its glass ceiling too. Down there, a woman is either arm candy or sex for sale unless she's smart enough to do it on her own. The first one who tried to treat me like sex for sale never bothered a woman again. He had a boss, of course, but I stood up to him too. Heart pounding, I marched straight up to him, put a gun in his face and said, 'We deal, or one of us dies.'

"There were half a dozen guns pointed at me by the time I finished, but boss man was impressed. From then on I started getting real work, the kind of work they could only send a woman to do. That's when I found out how profitable killing people could be and I've been doing it ever since, including that doctor. Turns out, he was the one who committed suicide. That's what the authorities said so it must be true, right?"

There's another silence, a gathering of what might be storm clouds while he digests it all. With nothing more than hope left, there is nothing to do but wait, until he says, "So . . . couldn't you have paid for your own surgery, what with all that money you made?"

"I did. A body like this doesn't come for free, y'know. As for going back, what would've been the point? I can't exactly grow a new pair so I decided to make the best of what I had and buried everything else, until you came along."

"Until I came along, huh? So what were you trying to do with that then? If what you got ain't real, what was that all about the day you took me home with you? Was I supposed to end up gay in a dress or out of it?"

"I wasn't trying to make you gay. I was drunk on wine and power, nothing more. I did it because I could."

"Really." He lies down again. "Because it sounds to me like you were trying to do to me what they did to you. And I thought *my* life was all messed up."

***

Morning comes. We've slept side by side on the ground. That wasn't meant to happen, but there it is. If anyone had come along, they might have thought we were dead, or maybe a couple of abductees dumped here after the aliens were done with their probings. That, we could certainly do without. Enough people are looking for us without having them on our case as well. My God, listen to yourself. One night under the stars and suddenly the entire universe is after you. Get a grip. No one out there gives a damn.

The hard ground we've slept on makes standing rough, but Angie brushes it off as easily as he begins to brush dirt from his clothes. Well, he is practically half my age. He also seems to be entirely unconcerned by last night's confession. He is as resilient as he is forgiving, or was, before he got shot in the head. Throw almost anything at him and he just shrugs it off, like me making him wear a dress. How different my life might have been if his ability to forgive had been mine.

Whatever. It's too late now, and there's dirt that needs brushing from the parts he can't reach.

"Morning, babe. You ready? Because we've got a big day ahead of us."

"Yeah? Why's that?"

"We're almost there. The next stars we see will be in a Mexican sky. Everything will change for the better then, I promise."

"Great." He starts to brush dirt from my back. "So do we get any breakfast first? I could eat another dead cow, and probably a wildebeest as well."

"So could I, so the sooner you're finished, the sooner we're back on the road."

That hurries him along and a couple of hours later, we're in Tularosa outside a lonesome sandwich joint, not much more than a large hut in the middle of a vast parking lot. This time in the morning, we're the only vehicle there. That doesn't mean he can't find more trouble to get into.

"No wandering off, okay? Whatever happens, whoever turns up, you stay in the vehicle."

He gives me a salute. "Okay, Mom. Now go get some food before I starve to death with all this neglect."

"Love you too, sweetheart. Be back soon."

A few minutes later, he's still sitting there, wearing a smile that's pure innocence. Silently we eat, with me watching traffic go by. One of those vehicles is a cop. While Angie doesn't appear to have noticed, he's certainly got my attention. After the cop in Merkel checked us out, we were tracked down by my ex-coworker, but this cop doesn't slow at all. It's possible he hasn't noticed us, or our stolen plates, but still. A new vehicle, or at least some new plates, would be a good idea. Or we just keep moving. If he did make us, it's going to take time to get any kind of a response out here. We'll keep moving, only stopping for absolute necessity.

We finish up and move on, making Las Cruces by mid-morning. Absolute necessity grins up at me from the dashboard. Our tank is nearly empty. We have to stop. We come in on the 70, finding a gas station easily enough. This time, Angie is coming with me to pay.

We step inside, and he decides he wants some candy. Well, that's fine. It's better than trying to pick fights with strangers. Back outside, it's not so good. Angie points across the street to a truck in the parking lot opposite. "Who's that?"

There's a guy inside, just sitting there. He could be watching us. He could just be waiting for someone. Angie's made his choice and, like a dog on a scent, he goes, forcing me to drag him back. "Angie, no! We don't want—"

He turns an ominous glare on me. "But he's one of them! We gotta take him out before he takes us out!"

"My God, will you look at where we are? We're standing outside a gas station in the middle of a town. Do you want every cop in the place to come looking for us?"

"But—"

"But nothing! You don't even know who that guy is. Now get in or . . . I'll take your candy away."

He doesn't want to, but he can't help the grin that's creeping onto his face. "Wow. You're really scary when you're mad."

And don't you forget it either, kid. While he gets in, my eye wanders casually across the street. That guy is definitely watching us now. He could still be one of my ex-coworkers or no one at all. Whoever he is, he isn't doing anything more than sit there. That's good enough for me.

For the next halfhour or so we drive around Las Cruces, wandering through suburbs and commercial districts like we're looking for somewhere. Lost as we might appear to be, both of us are keeping an eye on the rearview as we look out for any sign we're being followed. There is none, but that doesn't put me at ease. Any pretense we might be heading for Canada disappeared long ago. The Deep Web, the Network, and anyone else they might have brought in, they'll all be ahead of us now, maybe even all around us. They could move in any time and finish it. They don't right now because we're in a large urban area with lots of people around and they don't want the attention any more than I do—or they don't know we're here and that truck really was nobody.

Going with nobody, we quit town. El Paso is closest, but El Paso is in Texas and we're not going back there. The next town west on I-10 is Deming. For about forty-five minutes, we're cruising and everything is fine. There's a fair amount of traffic, most of it big rigs. Then Angie starts to get edgy. He thinks he's spotted something. "There's a truck behind us. I think it's that guy from the parking lot."

A look in the rearview and it doesn't seem so certain to me. There *is* a truck behind us but it doesn't look like that truck. Angie isn't in an asking questions first kind of mood though. He's trying to climb out of his seat, to crawl in back where our arsenal is hidden under a blanket.

"What are you doing?" Watching the road, keeping us straight and trying to stop him all at the same time is not so easy to do.

"That guy's following us. We gotta take him out."

"So, what, you wanna start shooting people up on the interstate? Have you forgotten what happened outside Mustang? We're supposed to be keeping our heads down, not causing a multi-car pileup. Just sit down, okay? I'll know if we're being followed."

He sighs heavily because one day, the world will learn to listen, y'know. "Fine. Whatever you say. Some getaway this is."

Fifteen minutes later we reach Deming, taking the first exit. It's signposted to Columbus and the border, but we're heading on into the center of town. The truck stays on the interstate. Angie answers my triumphant little smile with a sarcastic grin, then stares out at all the RV parks we're driving by, one after another of them.

A second signpost points us to Columbus and the border again. Since it's nearly midday, a last meal north of the border seems like a good idea. We find a place just beyond the next junction off I-10, on the corner of our road south. For a lengthening moment we sit, with me trying to decide whether or not to take him in or just get takeout. He seems relaxed enough. So long as he's kept occupied and away from other people, we ought to be fine. Besides, his patience is running out and that's definitely not good.

"Well? Are we going to eat or not?"

A few minutes later, a window booth well away from anyone else also allows us to talk freely.

"Sorry if this getaway isn't exciting enough for you, but, you know, it's the ones who go looking for trouble who get caught."

That earns me maybe an attempt at a shrug. He's more interested in looking out the window.

"Oh, come on, baby. We're that close to being home free. You gotta be happy about that."

Not even a shrug this time. He's still more interested in something out there. Following his gaze shows me nothing out of the ordinary. Maybe he's just bored.

"Look, when we get to Mexico, I'll take you out into the desert and you can shoot up anything you want. Cactus, lizards . . . just don't kill anyone. We don't want the Federales after us as well. After that, we can go anywhere, find a place to live, do whatever you want. There really is no limit. We could even go into space if you wanted to. You want to see a UFO, don't you? Well, what better way to do it than by becoming an astronaut? We'll have to take you to a hospital first, of course, have a proper physical done. Astronauts have to be super-fit, what with all those g-forces to survive."

That gets his attention, just not in a good way. "You still think I'm sick in the head, don't you? You still think I'm some kind of mental illness that needs to be drugged up so I'll sit quietly and be good."

A little bit of me wilts inside because, apparently, everything is now suspect. Everything is a personal attack no matter how innocent or well-meant it is. "Angie, we're not having this argument all over again. I'm just worried about you. You're so . . . up and down lately. I just want you to be happy, y'know? Not always flying off the handle at nothing."

"Nothing?" He points out the window. "You think that's nothing?"

Across the parking lot, on the other side of the street, is a truck that wasn't there when we arrived. It's not the truck from Las Cruces or the one on I-10, but it is another truck, just sitting there minding its business right where we happen to be. People have been taken out for less than that, and not so very long ago either.

"Come on, baby. Let's go. There's a three-course meal with all the trimmings waiting for us in Mexico City. Just don't do anything stupid."

Dropping the last bit of his burger, he rises with me. My arm wraps around him, just to be sure, and we walk out. We're not a pair of gun-toting psychos. We're just a mom and her son returning to their SUV. As we separate, everything's good. All we have to do is get in and we're gone.

Until, just as the ignition is about to be turned, he walks by and the AR-15 is in his hands. There isn't even time for me to get out before he's firing a burst at the truck across the street. Bullets pepper it from tail light to cab, only just short of where the driver's sitting, and he's not waiting around for a second helping. Leaving skid marks and the smell of burned rubber in his wake, he's hightailing it down the street with Angie firing another burst after him.

"What the hell!"

"Just taking care of business." He meets my stare with way too much assurance. "That guy won't be following us anymore."

"You don't even know that guy was following us to begin with!"

"You don't know he wasn't. You're just finding fault. Now get the motor running while I take care of them."

He's going after the restaurant. Inside, instead of hitting the floor, people are standing with their phones out.

"Angie! No!" My lunge for the AR-15 is easily fended off. There's not even time for a second attempt. He opens up on the restaurant, shattering glass along its entire frontage and finishing it all off with, "Man, they'll be cleaning that up for days."

"Why?" Too shocked to do anything else, my hands are spread in disbelief. "Why would you do that?"

While he answers with nothing more than a big smirk, people inside the restaurant start moving. Some are covered in shards, others with cuts. At least he doesn't seem to have actually killed anyone, but that hardly makes any difference. Already, sirens are wailing in the distance. We passed a state police station on the way in. There has to be other law enforcement in this town, but my disbelief still has me rooted to the spot.

"What the hell are you waiting for, woman? Get in and get going!"

This is a dream. It has to be, one where all my control is gone and somehow he's in charge. There isn't even any way of arguing with him or any memory of how my hands come to be on the steering wheel.

Climbing in behind me, with the sirens coming ever closer, he bangs on the seat at my shoulder. "Drive, baby, drive!"

As he commands, we pull out of the parking lot and head south for Columbus. This could be a nice Sunday drive, with us just tootling along enjoying the scenery. It could be but for the sirens behind us, screaming like banshees in the expectation of imminent death, their eyes flashing red and blue in the rearview. To hell with that! We have to get out of here. We have to run for the border. My foot hits the gas and we're to hell and gone.

"That's right, baby." He's like some demented imp at my shoulder. "You take care of what's in front and I'll take care of what's behind."

Climbing over the back seat, he's about to make things a whole lot worse, if that was possible. It is because now things do get worse. A vehicle pulls out ahead of us. It's the sheriff, and he's trying to block the road. He gets out, shotgun in hand. He better not think we're gonna stop. No, he thinks he's gonna take a blast at us. Good luck with that because, even if you do shoot, there's no way you're going to stop us bearing down on you. With barely a second to spare, he leaps aside and our vehicle swerves, clipping his as we make a right turn.

The road we're on runs west through blocks of housing. Behind me, Angie is reveling in it as he shouts, "We got 'em all after us, babe, but don't you worry! I'll take care of them!"

My sweet girl was so pure and innocent. Now he's trading gunfire with a posse and all Mommy can hope for is that there aren't any stray bullets taking out neighborhood kids.

Out of the housing and into scrubland we run. At last, a road heads south. With what must be every lawman in Deming after us, we swerve again. They follow until Angie puts a burst into one of their grilles. That one leaves the road, steam pouring from his radiator as he crashes through a fence and comes to rest in a cloud of dust. The others fall back, disappearing in the rearview as they give up the chase. Maybe they're not up for it. Maybe they don't want to leave Deming. Maybe they just got orders.

While that troubles me, Angie doesn't care. He's having the time of his life, whooping it up like a true desperado. "See, baby, we're Monster Mom and Angel. They can't touch us!"

My thoughts are on the road ahead because there's no way state troopers would just give up the chase.

CHAPTER EIGHTEEN

L eaving the back road, for a few miles we run clear on a county road. Then we take a hard right, followed by a hard left, on through some fields and another hard right. State troopers do give up when they know we're running into a roadblock. There are two big, black SUVs and men in big, black sunglasses with what looks like military-grade hardware. We skid to a halt maybe a hundred feet from them. They look at us. We look at them. They don't open fire. That doesn't seem right. Everyone wants me dead. That's what assassin said. They're going to hunt me to the ends of the Earth, come through my front door or stand at the bottom of my bed and wake me up in the middle of the night.

While that puzzle is confusing me, Angie is at my shoulder, his hot breath in my ear, his voice an awe-filled whisper. "Shit, man. Are those real spooks?"

Yeah, and one of them is walking toward us. He holds up a hand. It's an invitation to parley. Let me guess. He wants to make me a once-in-a-lifetime offer: my very own private room in some distant land, just one private jet flight and there'll be nothing for me to worry about for the rest of my life. Nah, don't think so.

Shifting into reverse, we slew through a one-eighty turn while they're still standing there holding their agency-issued dicks. There's a back road ahead and to my right. As we accelerate down it, Angie opens up on them. They duck for cover but still they don't fire. This is getting curiouser and curiouser.

The road takes us dead south into the desert. If they're pursuing us, they're lost in our dust trail just as this riddle has me lost. The Deep Web just tried to make me an offer, but the Network said everyone wants me dead. That doesn't work unless this entire thing has become some sadistic little game of catch and release. Or it's all a kind of persuasion, behavioral manipulation. Work for the Deep Web and they'll keep me safe from the Network, except the Network works for the Deep Web anyway, so that doesn't add up either. Or it's something else—and the whole thing is just confusing the hell out of me. There's only one thing that seems certain. This party ain't over yet. The next surprise is out there and we can only wait for it to appear.

It comes in the shape of a small, black dot just above the horizon. It's making straight for us. Somebody's gone and got themselves a chopper. The Deep Web is behind us so it must be the Network. She refused our offer so you go get her. You're murder for hire. You created this mess. Now you finish it.

Whoever's giving those orders must control the Deep Web. He could be a politician, an out-of-control bureaucrat, or some sorry-ass billionaire who thinks he's the gatekeeper to all that's right and good because, y'know, he's a billionaire. It hardly matters. They're all psychos and sociopaths, and the blood never sticks to them.

The chopper comes closer. It's small; it appears to be civilian. It's Network for sure, probably with the directors watching. Their asses must be on the line too. The takeover may be done, but it could still turn hostile. Like Grigori, Mr. Sorry-ass wants to work with people who don't disappoint so save your skins by giving me hers. There may even be Champagne on ice with corks just waiting to be popped. Well, don't turn away, guys, because this livestream ain't over yet. The track ran out minutes ago. We're in virgin desert. It's as good a place as any to show all those backstabbing sons of bitches how they don't quite rule the world yet.

The SUV skids to a halt.

"Give me the AR." Angie doesn't want to. It's his favorite new toy. "Come on! We don't have time to play games! Now get underneath and keep your head down."

He obeys, leaving me to take up a position on the far side of the SUV from the chopper. The pilot is clearly visible now, looking all cool with his baseball cap, his sunglasses, and his big, fat headphones on. Behind him, perched on the edge of the rear compartment with his feet resting on a runner, is cool guy number two. He's got an assault rifle:

scoped, raised, and ready to fire. Zero points for style or imagination, guys, but then that just makes my job easier.

The chopper begins to circle. They're trying to get a shot on me. Keeping my head down, the SUV stays between us. Until one of us makes a move this is a stalemate, or until someone else starts shooting. Damn it! Angie's sneaked a gun out and he's taking potshots at them. He's nothing more than an irritation though, a mosquito buzzing at their ear.

We continue to circle. Angie takes a few more potshots. That's the thing about mosquitoes. Eventually, they drive you mad. The chopper wiggles where it's hovering. Angie must have gotten off a shot close enough to bother them. Shooter opens up on him, just a short burst by way of discouragement. A short burst from me answers him. The chopper wiggles some more. Shooter replies. Bullets rip through the SUV, peppering it with holes and crystallizing glass. Better luck next time.

Shooter appears to be shouting at the pilot. He wants to come closer or maybe circle faster. Either way, the pilot has his own ideas. They move around, slow and steady. Angie fires off a few more shots. He's really getting under their skin now. Shooter fires on him. This isn't discouragement anymore. This is kill the little shit territory. Wrong move, numb nuts.

My aim is good, my burst accurate. Shooter fires off a couple of rounds then goes limp, the assault rifle falling from his hands into the swirl of dust beneath the chopper. Damn him if he didn't get lucky too though, winging me in the shoulder. No time to waste on that. There's still a chopper to deal with that isn't going anywhere.

While the pilot is still figuring out why shooter isn't talking anymore, the AR-15 spits until it clicks. The chopper starts to spiral out of control. Round and round it goes, where it'll end, no one knows. Scrambling to join Angie under the SUV, for as much as that's going to protect us, we both wait for the crunch. When it comes, he grins hugely. "Man, that was something else. You just took down a helicopter, an entire freakin' helicopter!"

"Well, I'm glad you liked it. Now come on. We gotta move."

As I crawl out, my first thought is for my shoulder. It's a through and through with nothing major hit. There's blood and there's pain, but nothing that can't be lived with. My second thought is for their nice, shiny, and probably very expensive chopper. It isn't a complete write-off, but they're gonna need a flatbed and a couple of hearses to clean up the mess. Never mind. The directors can always console themselves with that Champagne, and then start running.

Angie crawls out behind me. He's still grinning from ear to ear. "Yeah. We just got us some spook ass, didn't we?"

"Sort of, but there are still eight of them behind us, and they're gonna be real pissed. So come on. We're like fifteen minutes from free and clear."

A quick check shows me he's unscathed. The same can't be said for our ride. Broken glass and bullet holes are the least of it. There are also two flat tires and a leaking gas tank. It's not going to get us much farther but at least it starts the first time.

With the AR-15 in his hands again and one of our last two mags, Angie climbs in back to keep watch on our rear. The Deep Web will be coming fast, faster than we can manage with two flats and my shoulder. Their ears are probably already burning with all the screaming Mr. Sorry-ass is doing. Psychos like that just can't handle losing.

On the dash in front of me is a handgun because who knows what's waiting up ahead. The border should mean border patrol, unless they're being kept out of it like all the other regular authorities.

About twenty minutes later, we make it to a road. It runs east to west, with a fence. On the far side is another fence with a gate leading onto a road through farmland. As we lurch toward all of this with the SUV on its last legs, Angie shouts to me. There's dust rising behind us. The spooks are in sight, and they're closing fast.

The SUV pushes partway through the fence. That's it. It's done. Before abandoning it, Angie quickly bags up our armory. Across the road and through the gate we run. We can see their SUVs behind us now, like angry beetles kicking up a dust storm as they scuttle towards us. We're running out of everything: time, space, and energy. There ought to be something deeply philosophical about that. Right now, my feet are too busy pounding dirt to think of it.

Through a second gate, we go. There are buildings up ahead, barns or warehouses, a large one and a smaller one.

There are also trucks parked just beyond them. No idea where the owners are, inside the buildings, or maybe out on the land. It doesn't matter. Behind us, the SUVs have reached the highway. One of them is tangled up in the fence, but the other one is already on the farm road. We race for the gap between the two buildings. The SUV swerves into the yard and slides to a stop behind us. The spooks pile out, but by now there's a pistol in both my hands. One of the spooks goes down. The other one on our side of the SUV scuttles around back of it, firing off a wild burst as he goes. There are now three of them behind it. Also, the second SUV has freed itself from the fence and is fast approaching. Something has to happen now before we're hopelessly outgunned.

"What the hell?" Some guy walks out of the big building to my left, shotgun in hand. It's a start. "Keys! Give me the keys, now!"

"Okay, okay." With two pistols in his face, the shotgun hits the ground. "Just don't shoot me."

Dangling the keys in front of me, he scuttles back into the building as soon as they're taken. At the same time, Angie fires off a burst. The spooks behind us are making their move, and the second SUV has slid to a halt in front of us. We're boxed in, caught like rats in a barrel, or so they must think. Not yet. That shotgun will do nicely. I scoop it up and make my own move, yelling at damn fool Angie. "Get under a truck!"

He runs and slides like he's scoring a home run. Good for him, and good for me too. That second SUV is opening up like Pandora's box but it's a sure bet there's no hope inside. Up in front of them before any of the spooks scrambling out can even think of taking a shot, my first blast takes the nearest one down. The next one staggers backward as he's hit, almost but not quite down. A second blast and he's done. Another spook runs around in front of the hood. He fires off a few rounds. Another blast takes him off his feet. As he screams, a fourth one appears around the back. He's firing too, until he runs into my fire. Mr. Sorry-ass should have sent more Network people to do his wet work because these guys didn't have a clue.

The others don't either. Angie is still firing and they're firing back, but no one is hitting anybody. My boy probably isn't even trying to, but it doesn't matter. All he has to do is keep them pinned until the keys fit one of these trucks. It better not be the one he's under because it's soaking up an awful lot of fire. It isn't, and the other truck fires up first time.

"Come on! Get in back!"

He's up. He's climbing in. The spooks are up too. Two of them are firing at us. Bullets zing around us, a couple of them coming through the passenger-side door. One showers me with glass. The other hits me in the thigh. In the back, Angie ducks hard and my foot hits the gas. The wheels spin, and we're moving.

Back on the farm road, we're bare minutes from safety. Behind us, the first SUV veers into view. Two of the spooks are hanging out of the windows, waiting only to come close enough. They're too late. We can make this. We can actually make this. Goddammit, no we can't. The brakes lock. The truck slides to a halt. Angie is still flat down in the back. Good boy. "Just hang in there, baby. We're almost home free."

With the AR-15 in hand, I take a knee at the rear of the truck, and not a moment too soon. The SUV is almost upon us. The spook on my side is already firing. His bullets sing around me, but he might just as well be blowing love hearts. Well, here's some loving of my own. The AR-15 sputters, emptying everything it's got at their nearest tire. It blows. The driver loses control. The SUV swerves. It tips and rolls, smashing over and over along the road, only narrowly missing us.

So much for the Deep Web; a damp squib if ever there was one. Seriously, guys, somebody should have trained you a whole lot better. Perhaps Mr. Sorry-ass should get on that, except he's probably way too busy chewing the carpet right now.

My shoulder hurts, my leg hurts, but that thought still makes me smile. "It's sunny skies from now on, babe. Just you wait and see."

The AR-15 drops into the back of the truck in passing. Angie's still keeping his head down, but that's okay. It's been a busy day and this old lady limping by is more than happy to let him lie. South takes us across a road and into Mexico, an arid emptiness we drive through for long enough to take us a good distance from the border. There's nothing they can do now. Even if they call out the Federales or the Mexican Army, by the time they get here, we'll be in Mexico City.

I pull up and call him from inside the truck.

"Angie. You can get up now."

Still, he doesn't move. He doesn't react to a sharp rap on the glass either. Damn. Now I'll have to get out and hobble back there.

"Come on, Angie. The fun and games are over. You can get up now."

There are two patches of blood on his back and a spreading pool of it beneath him. Oh God, no. "Angie!"

Scrambling up beside him and turning him over, my hand rests on his blood-soaked chest. "Angie? Angie, wake up." His eyes open. Their gaze is weak. "Angie, you stay with me. I'm going to get you to a hospital. You just stay with me, okay?"

He manages to smile his beautiful smile. "Hey, Mom. Are we there yet?"

"Yes, baby. We're there. We're in Mexico."

"Well then. I saved you, didn't I?"

His eyes glaze over, and he's gone. No, no, no! "Angie! Angie, wake up. We're free, baby. You can't leave me now, not when we have the whole world waiting for us. Angie, please come back to me. What am I supposed to do without you? Who's going to forgive me when I screw up? Who's going to tell me it's all right? You have to come back, Angie. You're the only one who can forgive me."

He doesn't reply. He's sleeping like a child, enfolded in my arms with his head resting against my shoulder. Useless caresses smear blood across his beautiful face but it's okay. Mommy will clean it up later. Mommy will keep you safe, just as she promised she would. No one will ever hurt you again. So sleep, my baby. Sleep.

***

"Hola, señora. Qué pasa?"

Eyes as dead as me wait for an answer. He's a big man, muscular, with short, black hair and tats creeping out from beneath rolled-up sleeves. He's wearing loose pants and a shirt with the top buttons undone. Beneath it are gold chains that complement his watch, his rings, and his gold teeth. He's cartel. He has to be. And he's the boss. A little way behind him, standing beside their bright, shiny trucks, are five more men. They all look the same: interchangeable enforcers, right down to their state-of-the-art weaponry. They could have been here for minutes or hours. It doesn't matter. Time has no meaning. This world has no meaning. They have no meaning. My gaze is blank, uncomprehending, because there are no words that will ever put this right.

He leans forward a little, taking a good look at Angie before he says again, this time a little more slowly, *"Hola, señora. Qué pasa?"*

He wants something. He's expecting me to say something. There is only this. "He's dead."

"Sí. This I know." He looks back along our tracks toward the border. "We heard gunfire. We came to see who the gringos were shooting at. What did you do, I wonder, that they want you dead, and how much might they pay to get you back?"

So we're down to talking money. It feels sordid, disrespectful. My Angie is still lying here in my arms and he wants to horse trade over him. Well, fine. The affront is enough to begin forcing me out of my despair, to begin dealing again. "I can pay far more than them. Get me to a hospital a long way from here and you can name your price. You can have this truck as well, just as a sign of good faith."

He nods slowly, looking the truck over with something like a scowl before shouting to his men, "Hey, *mis hermanos*. We got a gringo here trying to enter Mexico illegally. What shall we do, eh? Kill her, turn her in, or take her money?"

His men grin or chortle, but none of them says anything. Boss man will make that decision. "We can take the truck anyway, and the weapons, and everything else. As to the other: half a million US."

Only half a million, or maybe he thinks it doesn't matter. She can't pay so we'll just kill her and take the rest. Or, better still, we'll take her and sell her. That ought to bring in a tidy sum. Well, *chico*, you could have asked a million and it still would have been cheap. "He's coming too. I want to bury him properly."

He looks at Angie again. He's no more impressed with that than he was with the truck.

"If I don't pay you, you can bury me with him. Hell, you'd be doing me a favor. Plus, you get a nearly new truck, with US plates. Where's the downside?"

A few minutes later, our convoy is heading south. Beside me in our truck is one of his guys. Angie is still lying in back, now covered by a sheet. The terrain his guy is driving us through passes as if in a dream. My thoughts are only with Angie, my heart as broken as he is. From the streets of New York to a Mexican desert, this world, or fate, or God, or whatever you want to call it, gave me an angel and I destroyed him. My tears start to flow. They may never stop.

THE END